W. Chatterton Dix

A vision of all saints

and other poems

W. Chatterton Dix

A vision of all saints
and other poems

ISBN/EAN: 9783741107894

Manufactured in Europe, USA, Canada, Australia, Japa

Cover: Foto ©Andreas Hilbeck / pixelio.de

Manufactured and distributed by brebook publishing software
(www.brebook.com)

W. Chatterton Dix

A vision of all saints

A VISION OF ALL SAINTS.

A

VISION OF ALL SAINTS,

AND

OTHER POEMS.

BY

W. CHATTERTON DIX,

AUTHOR OF "ALTAR SONGS," &c., &c.

———

JOHN HODGES,

47, BEDFORD STREET, COVENT GARDEN, LONDON.

1871.

INSCRIBED

TO

SIR ROUNDELL PALMER, M.P., &c., &c.,

EDITOR OF "THE BOOK OF PRAISE."

PREFACE.

SOME of the verses in this book have appeared in various magazines and newspapers during the past ten years. They are reprinted in consequence of a wish expressed by many persons that these scattered lines might be gathered into one volume. There is, however, much new matter which, it is hoped, will not be unacceptable to those with whom the old has found favour.

For permission to reprint the pieces entitled *Night and Morning* and *From Sunday to Sunday* I am indebted to the courtesy of Messrs. Houlston and Sons.

I have appended a table of tunes to which certain of the pieces, partaking more or less of the character of a hymn, may be sung, a course which, I trust, will not be deemed presumptuous.

W. C. D.

Lent, 1871.

CONTENTS.

CONTENTS.

CONTENTS.

TABLE OF TUNES.

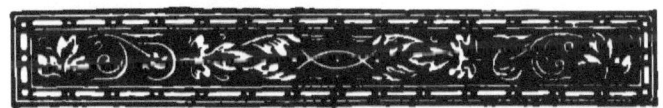

A VISION OF ALL SAINTS;

AND

OTHER POEMS.

A VISION OF ALL SAINTS.

WITH passionate pleading I make my prayer,
Lord Jesus, vouchsafe me an entrance there
Where the saints in robes of righteousness clad,
In perfect bliss shall for ever be glad.
Yet I am unworthy to enter in,
Thou knowest each act and each thought of sin,
The wayward will, the rebellions sore
Which keep me still kneeling at Mercy's door.

I watch the white-robed as they hasten past,
Say, did ever a sin its shadow cast,

Or did ever sorrow darken the brow
Which burns with the fire of saintliness now?

Answer me, answering, put me to shame,
Ye who fell down in the withering flame,
Ye who your being a holocaust made,
As the leaping fires on your bodies preyed.
Answer me, answering, put me to shame
Ye ranks of the faithful of deathless fame,
Prophets, Apostles, thrice glorious band
Whose sound is gone out into every land;
Answer me, answering, give me reply,
Who rather than fall, elected to die,
Heroines one in the smile or the frown,
Gems which shine forth in Virginity's crown.

Answer, ye valiant, faithful to death,
Curse ye my doubting, my impotent faith,
Tell of the strife and the pathways of thorn
Leading, through darkness, to Orient morn.
Ye prayed and many a victory won,
The law was obeyed and Commandment done;
Ye took up the Cross, and with eager breath
Followed your Lord both to prison and death;

O chosen of God, ye have sown in tears,
Kept your patient vigil of weary years,
And now ye shall reap in joy for reward,
The Joy of Jesus, the Joy of your Lord.
Ye spake words of peace, but of battle heard,
Ye blessed, but won only the cursing word,
And yet amid all, your pleading was still
To learn and to suffer your Father's Will.

O must I always a suppliant be,
With mercy my constant and changeless plea,
Only the gate of God's glory behold,
And still kneel on in the darkness and cold?

" Silence !" (the ear of the Master is won,)
" Thou art not yet perfect, My child, My son ;
Thou hast much to do, ere thou for reward,
Shalt possess My Joy, the Joy of thy Lord.
Nor art thou in darkness and gloom of night,
See, forth from Heaven's portals gleam warmth
      and light,
As bridal souls to their triumph go in,
The victor's crown and the guerdon to win.
Thou hast more of sweetness yet to refuse,

And more of sharp bitterness yet to choose,
And things best beloved to count but as loss,
For the sake of My thorny crown and cross.
The years are grown weary, the watching long,
Thou thinkest the Narrow Way must be wrong:
Thy faith grows weak and thy coward-heart faints,
Thou art not meet for the kingdom of saints:
Thy hands must be nailed to the Cross with Mine,
And thy feet be fixed to the wood, yes thine,
Be crucified, son, for the love of Me,
Or the crown of the saints is no crown for thee."

The Voice was hushed, and I turned me to pray
For grace still to keep to the Narrow Way,
And praying, I sought the trees of the wood,
And felled for my cross the tallest I could.
With many a blow I smote its rough face,
And hailed it the throne of my own disgrace,
Couch where the body of death should recline,
And the brow be torn with the crown of spine:
And I got me nails for my hands and feet,
And vinegar and gall for chalice sweet,
And I prayed to Christ, of His Mercy free,

That my sins might nail me fast to the tree,
And that then I should die, and wake at last
To the joy of those whose trial was past,
And with bridal souls, for my great reward,
By my cross thus gain the joy of my Lord.
I watched the white-robed as they hastened past,
I saw where the sin a shadow had cast,
Saw how deep sorrow had clouded the brow
Which burned with the fire of saintliness now :
I watched how they gained rejoicing and song,
Through much tribulation, through warfare long,
Through patient endurance, through hate and loss;
The crown of the Saints was won by the Cross.
I saw the marks received in the strife,
The scorch of the flame, the scar of the knife ;
The princes of earth are those conquerors blest
Who enter with joy the City of Rest !
And yet I a suppliant still must be,
Though I frame my cross from the forest-tree.

"Silence !" (O Voice of the Master Divine !)
" My son, the Cross thou must carry is Mine."

IN THE HAND OF GOD.

WHAT are all these who have passed to their rest,
These of the Paradise-shelter possest,
Whose cry from the altar, like bells over snow,
Steals softly from out of the Paradise-glow?

O these are all they who have finished the strife,
Who wait, lamp in hand, at the portals of life;
Wait for pure light and the fulness of bliss,
The prize of their calling they never can miss.

There are our friends well belovèd of old,
Souls whom the Shepherd has gathered to Fold;
There, where no robber nor thief breaketh in
Sweetest contentment those folded ones win.

Safe from the darts which the enemy hurls,
Safe for the city with gateways of pearls;
Safe from the burden the flesh has to bear,
Safe for the province where foe may not dare.

Safe from all perils within and without,
Safe for the song which the vanquishers shout,
Safe from the passionate struggle, the fray,
Safe for the passionless life in that day.

Day of rejoicing, of perfected light,
Day which may never sink down into night;
Death shall be vanquished and sin's hateful stain
Never shall sully its beautiful reign.

Day of the ransomed, their hope, their desire;
Nine-fold battalions of spirits of fire
Shall sing thee, when prayer and high sacrament
    done,
Life never ending shall be but begun.

These are all they who have passed to their hope,
Never again with a foeman to cope,
Their arms laid aside, they find rest in the vale
Where none may surprise them and none may assail.

They wait for the King who is coming in might,
At evening, or cockcrow, or midst of the night;

For the Master whose Cross they have striven to
    bear,
For the crown and the robe which they yet have to
    wear.

Do they think, as the city of Refuge they win,
Of the falls which were theirs in the country of sin?
As they grow in the depth of the love of their Lord,
Do they fail at the thought of *their* gaining reward?

Does their love to His love seem cold and untrue,
The thought of that city as more than the due
Of those who full weary in time of the fray?
Ah! the Lover of souls loveth stronger than they.

The waters of comfort still flow in Christ's Fold,
And He, the Good Shepherd, will tend as of old;
Till full consummation of body and soul,
And all the redeemed be made perfectly whole.

HYMN OF THE ABYSSINIAN CHURCH.

How sweet Thy words, O Love Divine,
O Love, for sinners crucified ;
The ransomed souls, the just are Thine,
    Since Thou hast died.

The nuptial Feast of Heaven they chose,
Where death and sickness both are o'er ;
Yes, where the living water flows,
   · They die no more.

How radiant their latter end,
Whose day of death One beautifies,
Coming, His very own to tend,
    In Paradise !

TO GOD THE HOLY GHOST.

O HEAVENLY King, O Paraclete,
 Who fillest all in all ;
Spirit of Truth, of Wisdom sweet,
 To Thee Thy children call.

Treasure of Blessings pure and free,
 Of Life Bestower Thou,
The fading earth grows fresh in Thee,
 To Thee the haughty bow.

Come dwell within, and purge away
 The sins which stain the heart ;
And where we coldly love or pray,
 Thy Fire of Love impart.

Within Thy courts we sing to Thee,
 O Uncreated Light ;
Adoring there, we bow the knee.
 Supreme, Unconquered Might.

True Pilot Thou of those at sea,
    Sweet Guide of hearts distrest,
O bring us where our souls would be,
    To Haven, Home, and Rest.

For what, if here in holy Rite
    With joy we prove Thy grace,
Shall be our bliss, when, Matchless Light,
    We see Thee face to face ?

JUDGMENT AT THE DOOR.

God cometh, let the heart prepare,
Let all be swept and garnished there.

Not as the Babe of Bethlehem
He comes to doom, to diadem.

Not as the scorned, the crucified,
The Bridegroom seeks His waiting Bride.

With clouds He comes, and every eye
Shall see the Judge of souls draw nigh.

The trump shall sound, and cohorts bright
Will swell His train of wondrous might.

Behold He standeth at the door,
The Christ Whose pity we implore.

God cometh, let the heart prepare,
Deep let the Cross be planted there.

So when the Sign in Heaven appears,
The Cross within shall stay our fears.

Thus in that day of woe and dread,
O God, may we be comforted.

PATIENCE.

" IF Thou hadst come, our brother had not died."
    Thus one who loved, to One who came so late ;
Yet not too late, had she but known the fate
    Which soon should fill the mourners' hearts, with
        tide
Of holy joy.   Now she would almost chide
Her awful Guest, as though His brief delay
Had quenched her love, and driven faith away.
" If Thou hadst come," oh, could we only hide
    Our heart's impatience, and with meekness stay
To hear the Voice of Wisdom ere we speak.

    We mourn the past, the tomb, the buried dead,
And think of many a bitter thing to say,
While all the time, True Love stands by so meek,
    Waiting to lift anew the drooping head.

THE VOICE OF GOD.

A VOICE pierced through the silent dark,
  A sleeper quickly rose,
But mortal had not spake a word
  To break the lad's repose.

And yet once more the voice pealed out,
  And roused the sleeping one;
"I did not call," the old man said,
  "Lie down again, my son."

The lamp of God was dying out,
  Which burned before the ark;
The priest of God was waxing old,
  His vision dim and dark.

"Lo, here I am, for thou didst call!"
  The Voice had rung so clear,
That surely now the master spake,
  And wished the servant near.

Ah, 'twas no earthly voice that came
  To break the sleeper's rest;

No priestly call to midnight watch,
　Or rite which Heaven had blest.

Far other than we fondly think,
　The ways of God are found ;
He speaks within the heart, and we
　Hear but some outer sound.

We go to friends for friendly aid,
　We wander far abroad ;
We shun ourselves, and will not own
　The voice to come from God.

Or if we do, we turn again
　To sleep away our fear ;
O for the open heart, the faith
　Of childhood sweet and dear !

O for the linen ephod pure
　Which girt the saintly child ;
Some power to keep our footsteps right,
　Our conscience undefiled !

Be ours the true obedience,
　Which loves, and loving, fears ;
Be ours the cry of gentle faith,
　" Speak, Lord, Thy servant hears."

THE NAME OF JESUS.

NAME, all other names excelling,
Name of Jesus, fear dispelling,
Music in the heart of hearts,
Ointment for each wound that smarts,
Light which cheers the hour of gloom,
Life which springs in deathless bloom,
Noon which knows not waning ray,
Joy which never dies away.
O I sing Thee, Name most sweet,
Jesus, Jesus, I repeat,
Thinking of the manger-stall,
Reed and vinegar, and gall :
Mindful of the parting word
Which the Virgin Mother heard ;
Musing on the empty grave,
Victory, and power to save,
Conquest dread and state unknown,
Pleadings at the Father's throne.

All the wonders grace has wrought,
All the pardon love has bought,
All the light of Gospel Story,
Meet in Thee, Thou Name of glory!
Thee proclaim the Psalmist's measures,
Thee, the ancient Scripture's treasures,
All the holy Prophet-nation
Heralds Thee with jubilation,
While the new law clearer rings,
With the joy Thy mention brings.
O I sing Thee, Name most sweet,
Jesus, Jesus, I repeat.
How can I forget the strain
Which shall ease this heart of pain?
How pass by sin's antidote,
Water to the parchèd throat,
Vision to the sightless eyes,
Pledge of better Paradise,
Gate of new Jerusalem,
Peace and Joy and Diadem?
Boldness Thou when flesh is failing;
Courage when the heart is quailing,
Glory of the Hosts Supernal,

Vanquisher of might infernal,
Strength art Thou to quivering breath,
Help in life, and hope in death.
O I sing Thee name most sweet,
Jesus, Jesus, I repeat,
When the Jordan waves are swelling,
Falls the darkness none are telling,
Be Thou Pilot kind to steer me,
Master of the vessel near me,
Anchor sure within the veil,
Light when fiercest storms prevail ;
Be Thou compass to direct me,
Mail and armour to protect me,
Shield when deadliest arrows fall,
Name of Jesus, be my All ;
Port upon the Heavenly shore,
Joy and Crown for evermore !

THE PROPHECY AND THE FULFIL-
MENT.

Malachi iii. 1—5. S. Luke iii. 22—40.

HE Whom ye are seeking
Is suddenly coming,
The Lord to His temple,
He Whom ye delight in.
The day of His coming,
O, who may abide it?
And when He appeareth,
Who stand up before Him?

Like fire of refiner,
Like soap of the fuller,
Is He Whom the Prophet
With trumpet tongue heralds,
To sit as Refiner,
To purge as the silver
And gold in the furnace,
The children of Levi.

Then shall the off'rings
Of Judah and Salem
Be righteous and pleasant,
As in the years ended.
And He will come near you,
Come near you in judgment,
And be a swift witness
Against the impure ones.

Against the false swearers, .
Against the oppressor
Of hireling in wages,
Of widow and orphan,
Of him without father,
And him that perverteth
The rights of the stranger,
And fears not Jehovah.

Throw open the portals !
The Lord to His temple,
He Whom we delight in,
Is hasting in triumph :
And saints stand before Him
In day of His coming ;

And when He appeareth,
With canticle greet Him!

The Lord of the temple
Is He, Who in meekness
Is borne by His mother,
Saint Mary the Virgin:
Incarnate He cometh,
To purge as the silver
And gold in the furnace,
The called of His kingdom.

Redemption in Sion,
For those who have waited,
To-day is revealèd;
To-day consolation
For Israel breaketh,
The light and the glory
Of Jew and of Gentile,
The Christ, the Anointed!

Yes! He has come near us
To help the oppressed ones;
He calleth the weary

And those heavy laden :
"Come, I will refresh you!"
The Christ in His temple
Hath giv'n Himself for us,
A sweet smelling savour !

THE WAITING SAVIOUR.

SEE, Christian soul, thy Redeemer !
  He is wet with dews of the night ;
To His wounded Hand is fastened
  The lamp of ineffable light :
The seamless robe is upon Him ;
  The crown which the King wears alone,
He waits and asks thee to give Him
  Thy love in exchange for his own.

There in the chill bitter morning
  He stands at the door of thy heart ;
The long night through He has waited,
  And now He is loth to depart ;
Yet once again He is knocking,
  He has knocked so often before ;
Was ever love like to His love,
  And what could thy Lord have done more ?

Yet still the door is unopened,
  Still Jesus is out in the cold ;
Still must His voice be unheeded—
  The tale of His love be untold ?
New sins clinging closer, nearer,
  Which seem in their youth green and fair,
Sins unabsolved, but forgotten,
  Yes, *these* keep thy Lord waiting there.

How long wilt thou keep Him waiting ?
  The morning is coming on fast ;
What if He go with the dawning,
  And what if this knock be His last ?
With Hand uplift He is standing,
  His sorrowful Face turned away :
He is well nigh faint and weary,
  How much longer will Jesus stay ?

THE PEARL OF GREAT PRICE.

CAME a merchantman of yore,
Seeking goodly pearls to store :
One he found, and straightway sold
All he had, that one to hold.

But another Merchant came
Seeking pearls He knew by name,—
Seeking, gave His all for me ;
Bought His treasure on the tree.

Seek I many pearls to own,
These for crown, and those for throne ?
All I have I sell to buy
One I find so fair to eye.

This the pearl all price above,
And I know Who calls it Love :
Faith and Hope, bright gems they shine,
But the pearl is Love Divine.

I, too, now, for Jesus Christ,
Look within for pearls unpriced :
Hid in heart and stored in mind,
But the Merchantman must find.

Down beneath strong passion's tide,
Down where weeds of sin-growth hide ;
Scarce discerned from what is base,
Yet how sweet the hidden grace !

Seeking many, finding one,
Finding all, thus lacking none,
Hold I each possession vain,
If I only this may gain.

Toiling on in life's swift whirl,
If I find this goodly pearl,
Till time's Merchant own at last,
Heart, not hand, must hold it fast.

"I THIRST."

WEARY beside the well He sat ;
O who can tell but Jesus knew the thirst
Which yet intenser grew, when on the Cross
    For Him no kindly fountain burst ?

" I thirst," His spirit may have cried,
Thus long before the Passion-hour drew nigh!
Thirsting for souls who sought some cooling stream,
    Yet passed the Living Water by.

" Give me to drink."   Can mortal hands
Trembling with guilt, the thirst of God relieve ?
Can man, the gift of God on God bestow,
    And will the Giver aught receive ?

Yes ! Jacob's well is here, and Christ
Still asks from each, some lowly gift of love ;
Perchance that cup of water which shall win
    The blessing of reward above.

O who will stay with folded hands,
What time the Master on the servant waits ?
The well is deep, but deeper still the fount
  Of that pure Love, which love creates.

And while He waits He looks us through,
Reading each hidden secret of the heart ;
Or smites us by an unexpected word,
  Which makes the wondering spirit start.

But even while He smites He heals,
And while He asks a gift, Himself ·He gives :
The Well which springs to everlasting life,
  The Water which for ever lives.

THE HOLY ANGELS.

How blessed are the sons of God,
 They stand around the eternal throne ;
The vesture of their first estate
 Still clothes them, and immaculate
The stoles which never stain have known.

No mist obscures their steadfast gaze,
 No darkness comes to call to rest ;
No tears may ever dim the eyes
 Which see the hills of Paradise,
The many mansions of the blest.

Unbroken day the Angels know,
 They never rest and never tire :
They hear within that Palace bright
 The Wisdom of the Infinite, .
They touch the mount which burns with fire.

And yet they come to visit us,
   They leave awhile that holy place ;
Yes, ere we know it, to our side
   They haste, those spirits glorified,
To win us by their heavenly grace.

We are as pilgrims on the road,
   We storm the pass and scale the height ;
But like a sparkling diadem,
   The city of Jerusalem,
Full soon shall break upon our sight.

We are as voyagers on the deep,
   Scarce for an hour the storm-blasts cease ;
But soon will fairer winds prevail,
   Stars will shine out, and we shall hail
The One and only Port of Peace.

The Angels are about our path,
   We seem alone, it is not so :
At home, abroad, on land, at sea,
   We have the Angels' company,
Earth gleams with all unearthly glow.

Surely to every faithful heart,
  Shall come a vision bright and fair,
Like Jacob's ladder soaring high,
  With countless bright ones of the sky
Ascending and descending there.

Whom the good Angels serve we love,
  Our Love, our Light, our Life, our All;
Links in the golden chain they are,
  Which binds us to our home, though far
We wander from Love's gentle call.

Let us not wander farther still,
  The pilgrimage will soon be past,
And holy Angels line the road
  Which leads us to the mount of God:
Sweet Spirits bring us there at last!

EASTER STANZAS.

To our Monarch, Christ, be the praise to-day,
Unto Him Who hath set His people free ;
The tribes of the Lord have passed through the flood,
Their foes overwhelmed in the depths of the sea ;
With His own right Hand and His holy Arm,
Hath He gotten Himself the victory.

The enemy said, " I will overtake,"
But horse and rider sank down like a stone
In the surging tide, when the parted floods
By the Lord of Hosts were together thrown :
With His own right Hand and His holy Arm,
Hath He gotten Himself the victory.

The enemy said, " I will cast them down
To the lion's den, to the sevenfold flame :"
But the Angel saved from the lions' mouths,
And a cooling wind to the furnace came.

3

With His own right Hand and His holy Arm,
Hath He gotten Himself the victory.

The enemy said, "I will bind in chains
Th' imprisoned souls in death's domain,"
But the Lord of Life led them forth in light,
And the bound of Hades were free again :
With His own right Hand and His holy Arm,
Hath He gotten Himself the victory.

Glory, thanksgiving, and honour, and might,
To the King of Kings from His servants be :
Through the grave and gate of death He has passed,
From the bonds of sin His own to free :
With His own right Hand and His holy Arm,
Hath He gotten Himself the victory.

EPHPHATHA.

LEAD us aside, we would not ever stay
    In pleasure's gilded haunts, but pass away,
    That we may hear more clear Thy heavenly
        Voice;
Too often we have sought the world's false glare,
Too often shunned the solitude of prayer,
And thrusting Thee quite out, thought we had
    made a goodly choice.

Perchance in some tremendous hour,
    Thou wilt deprive us both of pride and power,
    And make us on some tearful bed lie down;
Still Thou dost lead aside, and pain is sweet,
If we but kiss Thy wounded Hands and Feet,
And on our pillow for companion have Thy thorny
    Crown.

Lead us aside, over the holy dead
 It may be that we stand, and idly shed
 Tears which both dim our eyes, and shut
  out Heaven :
Give us to see the Resurrection Light,
And ere our wavering faith shall quite take flight,
To pray beside the open grave that strength to us
 be given.

Like him of old we come, O Lord, to Thee,
 Both deaf and dumb he was, and so are we;
 Good Master, now put forth Thy healing
  Hand ;
Our ears, O Lord, unstop, our tongue untie,
And make the powers of ill and darkness fly
Before that sigh of Love, the Ephphatha of Thy
 command.

ONE STAR DIFFERETH FROM ANOTHER.

THE stars above our head
    In divers orders move,
So God's elect, in divers ways
    The joys eternal prove.

Where all are crowned with bliss,
    Some, special glories know ;
For wheresoe'er the Lamb doth lead,
    The virgin souls may go.

And what to them He shows,
    Or what new wonder tells,
As far transcends our powers of thought
    As this star, that, excels.

And thus it is on earth
    With us who wage the fight,

Strong, giant-souls the world must see,
   But some strive far from sight.

Some in their stately march
   Strive out both clear and fair ;
And some so pale, that in our pride
   We think no light is there.

Yet lowly souls live on
   Like flowers in hidden sod,
Whose perfumes tell the secret place
   Where they reveal their God.

The meek shall gain the crown,
   The strong of heart reward ;
And this to all, the Joy of joys,
   That they shall see their Lord.

Thou, Who all hearts dost guide,
   Grant us thine aiding grace,
That we may tread the lowly path,
   Or take the hero's place.

O Trinity most Blest,
  This prayer we lift to Thee,
That we, who worship now by faith,
  In Heaven Thy Face may see ;

That when our race is run,
  And all the strife is o'er,
The lowest place to us be given—
  'Tis all we dare implore.

THE BRIDEGROOM COMING AT MID-NIGHT.

DARK fall the hours this winter-tide,
Strange silence reigns on every side,
    And day seems wrapt in gloom,
Save few short hours, which all too brief,
Light up bare tree and fallen leaf,
    Then fade in hapless doom.

Now let each lamp be burning bright,
Lest, unaware, the sudden night
    Enshroud us in the dark,
And we in vain, through snow and cold,
With wavering feet, seek out the Fold,
    And Love's all-sheltering Ark.

O silent hours of wintry days,
From summer's joy and golden rays,
    From autumn's harvest song,

We turn to you, for ye reveal
The waiting Bride, and make us feel
    The Bridegroom comes ere long.

S. MARY MAGDALENE.

Dear saint, we love to think of thee,
  For tears have made thee pure as snow;
And Love, compassionate and free,
  Has come to change thy life of woe,
And make thee reign a very queen
Of penitents, O Magdalene.

Thou lovedst much, and Love Divine
  Thy many sins did all forgive,
That thou, hewn out of sin's dark mine,
  A jewel in Love's crown mightst live;
That thou, once outcast of the street,
Shouldst meekly wash the spotless Feet.

O what a life of holy tears
  Must that new life have been to thee:
Thy heart so full of joy, that fears
  Must oft have come its guests to be;
Now, thoughts of all the hateful past,
Now, hopes of pardon wrought at last.

Meek patience thou hadst truly learned,
   And all self-pleasing cast away :
When stronger hearts had coward turned,
   Close to the Cross thou yet wouldst stay :
Among the last to leave Thy Lord,
Thou penitent by Love restored.

O sisters good, we pray for you,
   Who, cross in heart, and heart in cross,
Travel the busy city through,
   If haply ye may help the loss
Of those, who lost to woman's shame,
Yet bear, dread thought, a Christian name.

Ye toil in faith that some ye win
   May know the joy of Magdalene ;
That after years of wearying sin,
   They too may gain a rest serene :
Finding on earth, a place for tears ;
In heaven, an end to shame and fears !

THE LILY AND THE PASSION-FLOWER.

SORROW and joy in one brief day are met ;
    The Mother and the Child,
    The Undefiled ;
Sweetly Saint Gabriel's voice rings out, and yet,
    In tones more wond'rous still,
    Sounds forth th' Eternal Will.

The Seven Last Words are dying on the air,
    And haply Gabriel stays
    In dread amaze,
Close to her side, whom woes have made more fair,
    Than when she knelt, and heard
    His " Hail !" and gracious word.

O day twice blest, such mysteries to teach,
    Too short for human mind
    Love's depth to find,

And all too brief, wherein Love's height to reach :
    God, come as Babe to lie,
    As Very God, to die.

The Bride, with blossoms which she loveth best,
    To-day entwines a wreath
    Of life and death.
" Ave !" she cries ; then, " Consummatum est !"
    Lily and Passion-flower,
    Her pure, unfading dower.

Good Friday and Lady Day, 1869.

THE HOUSEHOLDER SENDING FORTH HIS SON.

A CHRISTMAS RHYME.

NIGHT was resting on the people, sin was out upon
the world,
Darkness, ere the prince of darkness, from his citadel
was hurled,
Ere the Prince of Peace, His standard o'er the
realms of strife unfurled.

Heathen madly raged with heathen, each with vain
imagining ;
Brother hated, slew his brother, king went out to
war with king,
Till all ill abounded, and the dove of
at length depth
peace too'

All the nations sat in darkness, loving best the veil
of night;
God they would not own as Ruler, so they put
Him out of sight,
Then the flames of Hell they quickened, trampled
on the true and right.

Thus the vineyard God had planted very good from
east to west,
Wicked husbandmen had ruined, eating, drinking,
taking rest,
Cursing with their lusts and passions what the
Householder had blest.

He had hedged about the vineyard, dug the wine-
press, built the tower,
Let it out and given orders, "Thou must serve and
thou have power,"
So that He of fruit might gather treasure in the
vintage-hour.

One by one He sent His servants till that hour
should fully come;

Some they beat, and some they stonèd, shame-
fully entreated some,
They whose hearts were set on idols, gods they
fashioned, senseless, dumb.

Last of all, the vineyard's Ruler when the num-
bered days were run,
Thought upon His loving-kindness, sent the Sole-
Begotten One,
Sent His best Belovèd, saying, " They will rever-
ence My Son."

Thus the Father in His pity, healed the world by
guilt opprest,
Gave commandment to the Lowly, bade her tabernacle rest,
He Who made her, Israel's Lily, slumbered on her
spotless Breast.

O, the mystery of mercy ! To the Vineyard comes
the Heir,
Leaves the Father's many mansions, faithless husbandmen to spare,

Clothes Himself with human nature, deigns our
very flesh to wear.

Heir of all things, we adore Him, Whom the
wicked madly slew;
" This the heir, come let us kill him," thus of old
that godless crew
Cast Him out the Father sent them, thus they
paid their Lord His due.

———

Fair the Vineyard which the Ageless purchased
with His own Right Hand,
Where the husbandmen of Jesus in the place
appointed stand,
Some to sow, and some to gather, some to break
the fallow land.

Hedged about by Law and Prophets, this Inherit-
ance Divine;
Deep therein is dug the wine-press, whence flows
Precious Blood for wine;
There the Tower of Ivory glitters, of Incarnate
Grace the shrine.

4

There the four-fold river waters with its crystal
　　stream the ground ;
Purest gold and precious onyx in its hidden depths
　　abound ;
There, or good for food or pleasant, every herb
　　and tree are found.

Thus the Lord our God hath planted eastward in
　　the Realm He made
Garden, unto which He sendeth, born to-day of
　　spotless Maid,
Him Whose light the ancients longed for, Him for
　　Whom the prophets prayed.

Where are springing thorns and briers, He will
　　make the curse to cease ;
Are there captives fast in fetters ?　He will give
　　the bound release,
Unto men of good-will, saying, "On the earth be
　　good-will, peace !"

Surely now the world will greet Him, Heir of all
　　the worlds sublime ;

Times, they say, are bad, disjointed ; He is come,
    the Lord of Time ;
Men, they say, have grown more evil ; He can stay
    the march of crime.

Do the hours of toil wax longer ?   He will share
    our weariness ;
Are there hands uplift to curse us ?   His are lifted
    up to bless ;
Are there words of hate about us ?   His are words
    of peacefulness.

O how happy the hereafter, when the better Eden
    gained,
We look back upon the vineyard where the labour
    was sustained,
One hand working, one hand grasping weapon
    while a foe remained !

Peace ! the Will of God the Father, as in Heaven,
    in earth is done ;
Peace ! the dreary years are ended ; Peace ! the
    days of strife are run ;

One the Song of men and Angels, "We will rever-
ence the Son."

Hid beneath His Fleshly garment, many a crown
and diadem
Brings the Heir this blessed morning, journeying
from Bethlehem ;
If He own us, if He bless us, who is he that dares
condemn ?

THE ENTRY INTO JERUSALEM.

JESU, Sion's King, we greet Thee,
On the Way of Sorrows meet Thee,
    Meekly coming unto death ;
In extreme humiliation,
Just and girded with Salvation,
    E'en as Zecharias saith.

King, how soon the cruel scorning,
Purple robe for mock adorning,
    Sceptre poor of bending reed ;
Then Thine infinite Affliction,
Bloody Sweat and Crucifixion,
    Thirst, and last dread Hour of need.

By Thy Precious Blood, good Jesus,
From transgression's burden ease us,
    By Thy Wounds, give Health divine,

And our lives vouchsafe to fashion,
By the virtue of Thy Passion,
    Into likeness unto Thine.

Thus hereafter may we merit
That glad City to inherit,
    Which the Cross, dear Lord, makes free ;
There, where nothing may afflict us,
Chant unending Benedictus,
    Palm and crown cast down to Thee.

THE EXPECTANT BRIDE.

Put on thy beautiful robes, Bride of Christ,
　　For the King shall embrace thee to-day ;
Break forth into singing, the morning has dawned,
　　And the shadows of night are away.

Shake off the dust from thy feet, Bride of Christ,
　　For the Conqueror, girded with might,
Has vanquished the foe, the dragon cast down,
　　And the cohorts of hell put to flight.

Thou art the Bride of His love, His elect,
　　Dry thy tears, for thy sorrows are past ;
Lone were the hours when thy Lord was away,
　　But He comes with the morning at last.

The winds bear the noise of His chariot-wheels,
　　And the thunders of victory roar ;
Lift up thy beautiful gates, Bride of Christ,
　　For the grave has dominion no more.

Once they arrayed Him with scorning; but see!
  His apparel is glorious now;
In His Hand are the keys of death and of hell,
  And the diadem gleams on His Brow.

Hark! 'tis her voice: "Alleluia," she sings,
  "Alleluia, the captives are free,
Unfolded the gates of Paradise stand,
  And unfolded for ever shall be."

Choir answers choir, where the song has no end,
  All the Saints raise Hosannahs on high;
Deep calls to deep in the ocean of love,
  As the Bride lifts her jubilant cry.

THE GOOD PHYSICIAN.

THE Balm of Gilead, Jesus Christ
Keeps stored His Treasury within,
To cure the leprosy of life,
To soothe the smarting wounds of sin.

There, chalices of healing stand
To cheer the weary souls and faint,
Filled to the brim by Love Divine ;
And cures for every heart-complaint.

The fires of passion, fever's force,
Fade at the Healer's gentle word,
And in the soul, so wild before,
The peaceful, still, small Voice is heard.

The Holy Mother comes to pride,
And meekly shows her lowly grace,
And selfishness and coldness flee
Before the lov'd Disciple's face.

And cowardice forgets its fears,
Shamed by the Martyr's dauntless heart;
And worldliness, her cares, to choose
For Jesus Christ, the better part.

Thus, Good Physician, Thou dost aid,
Most by Thyself, yet still by these,
The soul that looks to Thee for life,
And from its sin-wrought sickness flees.

The plagues of Israel die away,
Touched by the Royal Healer's Hand:
The lepers cleansed, the dead upraised,
Around the Cross rejoicing stand.

And bitter though the med'cine prove,
And sharp the scourge that works the cure;
How sweet the bliss Christ's loved ones win,
The true, the penitent, the pure!

THE TRANSFIGURATION.

FIRST came the hour of prayer,
　　Calm in the mountain-air,
And then with sudden blaze the glorious sight ;
　　Yet proud of heart, wouldst thou
　　Be blest on Tabor's brow,
Before thy patient prayers have stormed its height ?

　　Or thou hast slept perchance ;
　　Oh, for an Angel's glance,
The light to pierce, the Mystery to scan !
　　With Face of dazzling light,
　　In raiment pure and white,
With reverent gaze, behold the Son of Man.

　　Alas ! hadst thou but known
　　The vision to be shown,
How hadst thou strained thine eager, anxious eyes ;

Thy Lord transfigured there,
The while His unknown prayer
Rose, borne by angels, to the wondering skies.

How hadst thou watched! But now,
Before the Altered bow,
The Altered, still for thee, the very Same;
The Babe of Mary's knee,
The Christ to die for thee,
Clothed in a wondrous robe of burning flame.

From hidden grave afar,
From mystic fiery car,
The Lord of all the ages and of space,
The living and the dead
Brings to this mountain dread,
Bright with the radiance of Incarnate grace.

No thunders shake the air,
No lightnings strike despair,
Yet Law-giver and Prophet both are here;
God talks with men, and they
His glory see to-day,
Nor fall in dread amaze, for Christ is near.

Oh, in this awful hour
Of Rule and Kingly power,
The Lord of Glory surely speaks to them;
Nay, mid the shining light,
He tells of coming night,
Death that awaits Him at Jerusalem.

Proud heart, when soaring high,
Scaling the very sky,
Self-throned awhile in some seventh heaven of bliss;
Think thou with trembling breath
Of darkness and of death,
Thy Lord from Tabor's mount hath taught thee this.

And when the cloud is near,
And flesh shrinks down in fear,
As thou shalt enter on the dread unknown,
O Voice of Love be near,
Call through the cloud and fear,
Lead to the Mount of God, to Jesu's Throne.

ASKING IN THE SON'S NAME.

WE have not, Lord, because we ask amiss,
 But O wilt Thou not teach us how to pray?
What can we need or more desire than this,
 To ask in Thy dear Name from day to day.

With Voice unuttered in its awful might,
 With gentle strife in every chosen saint,
The Holy Ghost with force of Love and Light,
 Makes intercession when our wills are faint.

O Kind Redeemer, evermore impart
 To us that Comforter's abundant aid;
So tears will spring to ease the burdened heart,
 And faith make all our strongest foes afraid.

Then shall Thy blessing, like the gentle rain,
 Come down to cheer the souls that wait on Thee;
Love, waxing cold, shall warm to life again,
 And Grace and Sacraments will sweeter be.

Lord, who save Thee can know the mighty spoils
  Which one *Our Father*, breathed in faith may win?
What Crown for love, what end to all her toils,
  What Kingdom gained, or what the Joys therein!

THE CATECHISM.

AND wilt thou teach us, Mother dear?
We come to thee, yet come in fear,
   So much to learn, so little known;
Yet we will sit beneath thy feet,
To hear those words of wisdom sweet
   Which fall from thee, whose love we own.

And thou hast no forbidding voice;
Why fear we then to make our choice
   Of thee for ruler, leader, guide?
Is it because such depths of lore
As neither men nor angels store,
   Thou in thy scholar's books dost hide?

Or is it sloth which holds us back
From venturing the up-hill track
   Which saints, true men in Christ have trod?

O awful thought, that childhood's will,
May choose betwixt the good and ill,
   And learn of Satan or of God.

Now is the moment, mother dear,
When thou dost tell in childish ear
   The destiny of souls new-born ;
Forbid it that thy children choose
The evil, and the good refuse,
   And cast their birthright off in scorn.

THE CHURCH AS ESTHER COMING
TO HER KING.

Long years of fast and mourning,
   Long years of graces sweet;
Then, in her fair adorning,
   The Church her Lord shall greet,
Shall see Heaven's pavement glowing
   With colours richly dight,
The hangings proudly showing
   In purple, red, and white;
The marble pillars gleaming,
   The gold and silver sheen,
And crown, which brightly beaming,
   Shall deck her brow as Queen.
Like Esther, she, elected,
   Waits till the Bridegroom calls,
In Him complete, perfected,
   To more than Shusan's halls.
And days of grief grow sweeter

At thought of blessing won ;
She knows Who wills to greet her
At rising of the Sun.
And though she watch in sorrow,
At dawn her heart shall sing ;
To-day, in tears, to-morrow,
Companion of the King.
Then she, in raiment splendid
With divers colours wrought,
To Him, her exile ended,
By angels shall be brought.
To her He will deliver
His Sceptre to embrace ;
Her every sin forgive her,
Her every stain efface.
His favour she shall merit,
And at His own Right Hand,
Vesture of gold inherit,
And there for ever stand.
Hers then all regal treasure,
And in her beauteous grace,
Shall Christ, the King, have pleasure ;
O vision Face to Face!

BOLDNESS IN CHRIST'S SERVICE.

WHO the foe Christ's servants daring,
　　As for Him they gladly fight?
If He for us, who against us?
　　Who shall put our ranks to flight?
Let the heathen rage in madness,
　　Let their cohorts death prepare:
God of battles, Thou wilt aid us,
　　Thou wilt own the arms we bear.

See! our banner proudly floating,
　　'Tis the Cross which makes us brave:
Yes, the crimson Wounds of Jesus,
　　In the hour of trial save.
Who defy the Master's Kingdom?
　　Who insult His awful throne?
Not the world, the flesh, the devil,
　　But the hearts who Him disown.

These are they who walk not with Him,
   These with coward-heart who fail:
These, who in the hour of trial,
   At the sight of suff'ring quail:
Hark! His words peal out like thunder
   Borne from lips of Love Divine,
"What my own, will you refuse me?
   When I ask your love for Mine."

"Never, Lord, and Master, never,"
   This the loyal servant saith:
"Save from foe and faithless service,
   Keep me true in life and death:
Then let all Thy judgments vex me,
   Storm and tempest strike me down,
"If through these I win the blessing,
   If through these I gain the Crown."

"IN THE PLACE OF THE TRAITOR"

A STAR has fall'n from Israel,
  Into blackness of the night:
A guard betrayed the citadel
  For which he sware to fight:
The friend, whom the Master knew so well,
  With a kiss was the first to smite.

With "Master" on his lips he came,
  With a kiss for sign they knew:
"Whom I shall kiss, He is the same,"
  Thus, of the chosen few,
One let the prince of the world inflame
  To the work of the savage crew.

His house be ever desolate
  And let no man dwell therein!
His bishopric and high estate
  Henceforth another win!

The field of blood be the traitor's fate,
  For the dark offence and the sin !

———

Who fills the vacant throne ?
  Their guide who took the Lord
Self-stricken, overthrown,
  Hath perished for reward.
He by transgression fell,
  And, gone to his own place,
Another now must tell
  The Mysteries of Grace.

Matthias, thine the crown
  Which shines with regal glow,
Since Judas is cast down
  To depths of utter woe ;
The mantle thou didst wear
  Of him who sold the Lord :
Thou, glorious and fair,
  He, all accursed, abhorred.

Our lot is in Thy Hand,
  Chief Shepherd of the sheep :

If Thou dost call, we stand
　　A faithful watch to keep,
Thy work to undertake,
　　Thy Cross to lift on high,
To suffer for Thy sake,
　　If need be, e'en to die.

It may be called the last,
　　Yet Thou wilt own as first,
Forgiving what is past
　　Where tears of penance burst ;
Lest any with a kiss
　　Betray Eternal Love,
For silver pieces, miss
　　The golden streets above :

Lest any, once again
　　Put Christ to open shame,
Sin-pierce Him, wound to pain,
　　And then, for wages claim
The payment of the world,
　　The covenant of lust,

And at the last, be hurled
  From thrones unto the dust.

Lord, as the sworn and true
  Our names be ever known,
Or serving out of view,
  On an Apostle's throne :
Enduring, that we win
  The Guerdon and the Feast,
To which, O call us in,
  If last, yet loved not least.

THE BLESSEDNESS OF SERVING.

WHO stand supreme among the blest,
The first in Christ's great host confest?
Those lowly soldiers, who their Lord
Serve far from sight, from earth's reward.

They, like their Chief, content to serve,
Though inward strength for ruling nerve:
Leaders and guides with lion-heart,
Willing to play the servant's part.

" Who is the greatest at the Feast?"
The chief is now become the least,
The servant than his lord more great,
The lower than the high estate.

When forth from Wisdom's gate we go,
Where crowds are hurrying to and fro,
Over our souls, so heated grown,
The shadow of the saints be thrown!

Perchance, unseen by mortal eye,
Saint Peter gently passes by :
What if for wife, or house, or lands,
We spurn the Apostolic hands ?

Be ours to take the lowest place
And share with saints the saints' disgrace :
" As he that serveth," thus to gain
The kingdom where the meek shall reign !

SAINT THERESA.

TWENTY years of prayer unanswered,
　Years of strife and conflict keen,
Stern repulse and disappointment,
　Then the saintly life serene.

O how soon do we grow weary,
　Often asking the same thing,
Thinking not, that by our patience
　God our wants is measuring.

Yet we fancy, holy daughter,
　We were happy if like thee :
O so blessed, O so peaceful,
　If our lives as thine could be.

Thus too oft God's saints we value,
　Smiling on their happy end :
What, had they no foes to conquer,
　Heart to break, and will to bend ?

She whom Christendom remembers
  Seemed to know a perfect calm ;
And in love, rejoicing ever,
  Showed the world her victor's palm.

But the long, hard years of conflict,
  These all went before the crown
Which on earth to her was given,
  After many a casting down.

We pass by the long probation,
  Fast and watch and secret tear,
Which, transformed, to God and angels,
  Stars in crowns of saints appear !

LOVE AND THE PLACE OF REST
AFAR OFF.

HERE weary men know much of pain and sadness,
Wending their way to Zion, seat of gladness,
　　　　Where troubles cease :
Here, to their Rest, life's travellers are turning,
And wandering ones are penitently yearning
　　　　For Home and Peace.

Now the false deed and eager, vain relenting,
Some shameful sin, and bitter, sharp repenting,
　　　　Tears, prayer and fast :
Soon and for us, no room for supplication,
Prayer swallowed up in ceaseless adoration,
　　　　Heaven won at last.

The narrow way is dark, and foes offend us :
The warfare's mysteries well nigh transcend us,
　　　　Faith quails at sight :

But once the City gained, an end to weeping,
The Throne, the Crystal Sea, the censers sweeping,
    The Lamb our Light.

Love, her unworthy fears, her sighs repressing,
'Burns with the hope of endlessly possessing
    Her high desires ;
E'en in this vale of tears, afar divining
Jerusalem, and gloriously shining,
    Her gates and spires.

This is the Place of Rest she seeks for ever,
And seeking, though she faint, she falters never,
    But with her eyes
Firm fix'd, where dwells her Lord's eternal pleasure,
She prays, her heart where lies her highest treasure,
    For Paradise.

A CAROL OF THE RED SEA PASSAGE.

Lo! Israel's hosts from Egypt's coasts
  With song and dance come sweeping,
The Red Sea past, and Pharaoh cast,
  Where now the waves are leaping.

      God led them forth on foot,
        With glorious Right Hand,
      The very deep as on a heap,
        For them He made to stand.

Dryshod the tribes went through,
  In vain did foes pursue;
Not for that Godless crew,
  All night the east wind blew.

The Lord of Israel wrought
  His works of mighty wonder,
His arm salvation brought,
  And cast the tyrant under.

Madly the king essayed
  To follow and give battle,
Who in his ranks afraid,
  Or men, or neighing cattle ?

But their chariot wheels drave heavily,
  And the frantic steeds were down ;
The walls of the sea looked hungrily
  On the army God would drown.
The captains and mighty men grew mad,
  And the king was blind with fear,
Destruction met their lines at the front,
  And destruction swept their rear.
Commands were given, but not one was heard,
  Or none had heart to heed them,
The trumpet-blast rallied men aghast,
  No leader now could lead them.
Those men of blood quailed at the flood,
  The path of their foes' salvation
To them became contempt and shame,
  And a highway of damnation.
In vain the sword against the Lord,
  The hopes which His haters cherished,

6

A Carol of the Red Sea Passage.

The Prophet of God uplifted His Rod,
　And the king and his cohorts perished.

　　　Whelmed in the deep,
　　　Lost, overthrown,
　　　Down as a stone
　　　They sank in sleep!

"Sing, for the Lord hath done gloriously,
The horse and his rider are thrown in the sea!"

This glad new song sang Israel's throng,
　Their fathers' God upraising;
His mighty name for aye the same,
　Let all men now be praising!

　　　God led them forth on foot,
　　　With glorious Right Hand,
　　　From Egypt free, from tyranny,
　　　Into the Promised Land!

A GROUP OF VIRGIN MARTYRS.

I. S. AGATHA.

UNTO Jesus we sing,
  Our Redeemer and Lord,
Of all Virgins, the King,
  Their Defence and Reward.

What to them smile or frown?
  Jesus Christ they embraced,
That His glorious crown
  By their love might be graced.

Thus Saint Agatha keeps
  Sternest hold on her cross:
In her pilgrimage weeps,
  Counting all things but loss.

Life of Angels is hers,
  What though lover implores?
Only passion that stirs,
  Love which Jesus adores.

Welcome wounding and pain,
  Welcome Quintian's knife,
If through these she may gain
  Glad escape from the strife.

Hers, that love of the saints
  Which inspires the last breath
Love which fails not nor faints,
  For 'tis stronger than Death.

Unto Jesus we sing,
  Our Redeemer and Lord,
Of all Virgins, the King,
  Their Delight, their Reward!

II. S. FAITH.

SAINT Faith, her Lord, with latest breath
  Before her foes confessed,
Then meekly bowed her head in death,
  And gained the Martyr's rest.

Her life, her death, alike she gave
  To Him she owned as King:

A Group of Virgin Martyrs.

A life most pure, a death most brave,
  Accepted offering.

Hers is that little coronet*
  Which, over and above
The promised crown, Christ's virgins get,
  Reward of chastest love!

Of Virgin-Martyrs, Thou the Crown,
  O Lord, vouchsafe us grace
To welcome here contempt and frown
  Which win us Thine embrace!

III.   S. CECILIA.

Now in numbers soft and flowing
  Sing the Virgin-Martyr's fame;
Sweetest hymns befit her praises,
  Who hath music in her name;
Saint, who in the conflict conquers
  Through His might Who overcame.

* Bishop Jeremy Taylor.

She who makes her life another's,
  Dower mystical to choose :
She who gives herself to Jesus
  While the polished courtier woos,
Nursed in ease, in Roman softness,
  Say, will she the Cross refuse ?

Nay, the better part she chooseth,
  She elects for conscience' sake
Torments in the scalding water,
  This the couch she wills to make,
If through fire, and if through water,
  She to Song eternal wake.

Not the hour of mortal anguish,
  Scarce the branch of martyr's palm,
Shows the Church in pictured story,
  But the Saint in virgin calm ;
Notes divine her touch creating,
  And her voice uplift in psalm.

Thou Who givest palms to Martyrs,
  To the Virgins fair renown :

Grant to us with Saint Cecilia
   Here to bear the casting down,
So with her, we win hereafter,
   Recompense, Reward, and Crown.

So with her, the Song unending
   We uplift the Throne before,
Gone the night of our affliction,
   Trial and contending o'er ;
Past the altogether passing,
   Reached the one, abiding Shore !

THE PEACE OF THE CROSS.

THOUGH bitter be the med'cine,
  And arts of healing sore :
How strong the consolation,
  When hours of pain are o'er.

O Jesu, Good Physician,
  None but Thy sick ones know
How sweet the brimming chalice,
  Which takes away their woe.

The cup of this world's pleasures,
  For saints hath no delights,
For at the last it stingeth,
  And like a serpent bites :

But theirs the cup of blessing,
  By unbelief accurst ;
Sole draught, which, while refreshing,
  Intensifies their thirst.

"Watch thou, endure afflictions,"
 The message comes to them,
" Fight the good fight, be faithful,
 " Henceforth the diadem.

"Yes, Demas hath forsaken,
 "And friends are far away,
"This present world is evil ;
 " But I am thine for aye."

The world, nay friends, may cheat us,
 But how will sorrow cease,
If in our house One enter
 And say, " I bring you peace !"

TO THE BLESSED TRINITY.

THRICE Holy God, behold us now confessing
Thee, Mystery of mysteries, worthy of praise and
    blessing: .
    Standing afar we worship Thee, without the Holy
    Place
Where in fullness of Thy Majesty, Archangels see
    Thy Face.

    Past finding out, lo! prostrate we adore Thee,
As seeing Thee, Invisible, we meekly fall before
    Thee,
    And dare to take within our lips Thine awful
    Name, Most High,
Which the purest of Thine Angels cannot meetly
    magnify.

    When wilt Thou grant us of Thy grace and pity
To gaze on Thee, dread Three in One, within the
    Ageless City

Whose walls and towers and bulwarks in their
    golden glow are white
Through the brightness of Thy presence, through
    the burning of the Light.

There never more shall foe our peace imperil
Where the highways are gold-paven, the gates of
    pearl and beryl,
  All our sorrow be forgotten and sighing find no
    place
In the fullness of the Vision of the Glory and the
    Grace.

All, all is joy and holy high thanksgiving
Where Thou art throned, blest Trinity, Thou Light
    of all the Living :
  Where the censers of the Nine-fold sweep o'er the
    Sea of Glass,
More than visions of Earth's pilgrims in Thy pre-
    sence come to pass.

There the "Thrice Holy" evermore is breaking,
And thunders of Dominions, "Amen" are answer
    making

To the creeds of all the faithful, that chosen,
    royal Host
Which believes in God the Father, God the Son,
    and Holy Ghost.

Blessing, honour, might and praise for evermore
To Thee Whom the Angel-cohorts, with their faces
    veil'd adore :
    From Thrones, from Powers, Dominions, all praise
      to Thee be sent,
The Father, the Son, the Spirit, Eternal, Omnipo-
    tent.

MEMORIES AND HOPES.

How brief the tide of Paschal joy,
   How faint our Alleluias swell:
A sadness steals across our hearts,
   Whence, what it is, we scarce can tell.

The earth puts on her festal robes,
   The summer comes with golden hours,
And yet withal our spirits fail
   At thought of happier days, once ours.

Perchance forgotten strains come back,
   We sing and think to find relief,
But soon our voices die away,
   And we break down for very grief.

An Altar where we kneel no more,
   The calm of some remembered day,
Old hymns which we no longer sing,
   Old friends, old faces passed away.

Sad memories these, and yet so blest,
    They bind us to the happy past ;
We store them in our hearts, and pray
    For evening light to come at last.

But if some sin thus make us mourn,
    Then ere we see our Lord again,
Sorrow must fill our hearts awhile,
    And we must tread the path of pain.

A little while—how long, how short
    That little while, we may not know :
Too long for love to mourn her Lord,
    Too short for penance-tears to flow.

A little while, then grant us, Lord,
    The joy which none shall take away :
Joy of the peerless Easter-tide,
    Bright with the Son's abiding Day.

THE EMBRACING OF THE BODY OF CHRIST BY HIS VIRGIN MOTHER.

O THOU uncovered corse, Word of the Living One,
   Self-doomed to be uplifted on the bitter Tree,
Thereon to die, Thy patient Will, Eternal Son,
   And thence in Love draw all men unto Thee.

Which of Thy holy Members is without a wound ?
   The thorny Wreath Thy blessed Brow embraces
      fast :
No place whereon to lay Thee, weary Head, was
      found—
   But Thou shalt rest within a Tomb at last.

O Lips, which once with sweetest Words did over-
      flow,
   Fresh from sharp vinegar and bitterness of gall ;
O Cheeks, how often turned to many a smiter's blow,
   And spat upon in Pilate's judgment-hall.

By hands of men made helpless on the dreadful
    Beam,
  O Hands, of man creative, how were ye pierced
    through ;
Yet all outstretched, ye reach e'en Hades to redeem,
  And give the first transgressor help anew.

O Mouth all sweet, no guile was ever found in Thee,
  And yet, alas! by traitorous kiss wast Thou be-
    trayed ;
O blessed Feet, that walking on the stormy sea
  All water hallowed as the waves obeyed.

Where is the chorus of Thy sick ones, O my Son,
  All those infirm whom Thou didst heal, the up-
    raisèd dead ?
To draw the nails from Hands and Feet, there came
  not one
Of all the crowds whom Thou hast comforted ;

Only came Nicodemus, he who sought by night,
  And Joseph kind, whose rocky Tomb Thy Bed
    shall be,

Whither to sleep a Lion's sleep in awful might,
   My Son, how soon will they be bearing Thee!

Now Thou art borne to me from yon sharp cross of
         pain,
   And heavily upon these Mother-arms art laid ;
These arms which bare Thee long ago, and once
         again
   A lowly resting place for Thee are made.

I, who first swathèd Thee, Thy Grave-clothes now
         will bind,
   Giver of life, Thou liest dead before me now ;
Tears laved Thee at Thy Birth ; far hotter tears I
         find
   To wash the Death-drops from Thy pallid Brow.

High in these arms Maternal Thou didst leap,
   Thou Who wast born of me, this weary world to
         save ;
O bitter Funerals! that I who hushed Thy sleep,
   Must wail this doleful Passion o'er Thy Grave.

7

SIGNS AND WONDERS BY THE NAME OF JESUS.

In fancy for awhile I stand
   Beside the great sea shore ;
I hear the mighty, surging flood
   Of many waters roar.
I watch the curling wave-banks sweep,
   With crests of silver foam,
Now dashing on the cliff's rough face,
   Now leaping to their home.

A craft is plunging in the storm,
   Say, can she ride it out ?
Her sails are rent, her rudder gone,
   Her crew for succour shout ;
An Angel speaks, " By Jesu's Name,
   Now let deliverance be !"
And at his word, immediately,
   Sweet calm spreads o'er the sea.

*   *   *   *

A battle-field is in my view,
   And Wrong and Right are there ;
Close ranks of sturdy infidels
   Come forth Christ's Knights to dare ;
Those chivalrous who count it gain,
   And all things else but loss,
To die, if need be, for their Lord,
   And thus endure the Cross.

The heathen hosts are pressing hard
   On Red Cross Knight and lord,
Each strives as none have fought before,
   As none have ever warr'd ;
Good spirits turn each Christian sword
   To blades of living flame,
And victory is won by faith
   In Jesu's sacred Name.

*   *   *   *

Yet once again a strife I see,
   But no dark lines are here ;
Two, hand to hand, are combating,
   And one holds honour dear.

The sworn of Christ, he cannot hear
 The voice which lures to sin,
Though Pleasure sing with siren-notes
 The slave of Christ to win.

She comes with smiles, with shameless kiss,
 With hands that seem to bless ;
But poison is upon her lips,
 Her touch is bitterness :
Bright wreaths of gorgeous flowers she brings,
 The Crown of Thorns is best ;
Her songs are discords in the ears
 Which Jesu's Name hath blest.

  * * * *

I love the names of all the saints,
 I know their music well,
The canticles of those who won,
 The sighs of those who fell ;
Peter and John, and blessed Paul,
 And tearful Magdalene,
Teresa, Agnes, Margaret,
 And Mary, Virgin-Queen.

But, Name of Jesus, Thou dost break
   The hearts of very stone ;
Thou kindlest fires angelical
   About the Glory-throne ;
Ten thousand sinners flee to Thee,
   Ten thousand saints adore,
And all the heavenly hierarchies
   Uplift Thee evermore !

OUR FATHER IN HEAVEN.

WHAT though a father's heart grow cold,
   And love with life decay ?
Our Heavenly Father changes not,
   Nor turns His Face away.
And though a mother's long-tried love
   Forget the son she bore,
Not such the Love, which though unloved,
   Burns on for evermore.
O not from us, but from our sins
   God turns away His Face :
Even the very prodigals
   He takes to His embrace.
Is He our Father ? and are we
   So fallen, of Heavenly birth ?
Yes, for Eternal Love has bridged
   All between Heaven and earth.

Sin made the breach, but God destroys
  The gulf which none could span,
When men become the sons of God,
  Through God the Son of Man.
Our Father: so, then, not alone
  We lift our prayer on high ;
All Christians storm the Throne of grace
  With that one, common cry.
Our Father: then, as we love Him,
  We love who with us call,
Not few, at best most selfishly,
  But all, as He loves all.
Love still must win the world to God,
  To all things true and good :
The banner over us is Love,
  Love, badge of brotherhood.
The Love of God is God Himself,
  Our Father throned above ;
For he whom God Incarnate loved,
  Saith, "Children, God is Love."
Then when we love, we seem like Him,
  Nor is this all our boast :
He dwells in us and we in Him

Most, when we love Him most.
Our hearts a dwelling-place for God !
  The mind sinks down opprest
At thought of having Heaven within,
  Our Father for our guest.
We sound the depths of ocean's caves,
  We soar in upper air ;
Science puts out her hands to God,
  And work seems well nigh prayer.
We gird the earth with bands of thought,
  We stay the lightnings' flight :
Is man to be Omnipotent,
  Or mortal Infinite ?
No ! for this Earth with all her pride
  Breaks down dismayed, o'erawed,
Before the thought no mortal grasps,
  God, and the Love of God.

A MIDDLE-AGE REVERIE.

'TWAS of old a knight went out to fight,
   And he sware by the Lord of Hosts,
That his deadly foe should be lying low,
   Who had camped on his well-won coasts ;
And dared to stand with a haughty band,
   And to taunt with insolent boasts.

As a surging flood, the pride of blood
   Raged and stormed in the knightly breast :
His soul was on fire, and his new-found ire
   Tossed the mailèd coat on his chest
Like the angry deep, which cannot sleep,
   In its terrible, wild unrest.

When merged the night into morning light,
   The lord and his vassals had kept
Their vigil to God, ere they went abroad,
   And the women and children wept.

The Mass was said for the quick and dead,
  And swords from their scabbards out-leapt.

" Now whoso faints, by the holy Saints,
  Let him linger behind to pray ;
With the women and priest, he stands released,
  With women and priests let him stay :
Ye brave, upstand, with your swords in hand,
  Hark ! the trumpet calls to the fray."

They sprang to their feet, for the cause was sweet,
  'Twas the cause of their dear fire-side :
The foe was near, wife and children were dear,
  And the lover feared for his bride :
They sware to fight for God and the right,
  Those men of the olden-tide.

" When Mass is next said for quick and dead,
  Who will stand on this chauntry floor ?"
Thus the women sighed, and the children cried,
  " Will they not come back any more ?"
Mid women's fears and the children's tears,
  They passed out through the chapel-door.

The foe was sought, and at eve they fought,
  The knight and his foe face to face :
Who shall be cast when the battle is past,
  Whose banner be furled in disgrace ?
" The Saints give aid to the sore afraid,
  And our Lady help by her grace !"

　　*　　　*　　　*　　　*

    " Help to him who fails and faints,
      Victory, Christ, grant us this :
    Mary Mother, all the Saints,
      Ora pro nobis !

    Michael, wield for us thy sword,
      Crown our hearths and homes with bliss ;
    Scatter, break the hostile horde,
      Ora pro nobis !"

Thus, clear and strong, rose the holy song
  At the Vesper hour, for the band
Of the brave, who had gone their land to save
  From the touch of the spoiler's hand :
At their leader's call, forsaking all,
  In the face of the foe to stand.

What time they sang, the clarions rang,
   And the banners flashed in the sky,
And the warriors heard their Captain's word,
   As the last dread assault drew nigh ;
" Strain every nerve, and may Heaven preserve
   Those who keep what they have—or die."

The struggle began—strife man to man,
   And good blood encrimsoned the ground
Where, not long ago, in its golden glow
   The ripe grain was waving around :
Where, in scarlet hue, and softest blue,
   The poppies and corn-flowers were found :

Where children played, and bright garlands made ;
   O fairer the garlands won now :
A crown, a name in the story of fame ;
   A crown for the conqueror's brow,
A name, which should last, when, years gone past,
   They tell who were victors, and how :

Tell how the knight, grown ghastly and white,
   In hand to hand fight with his foe

Was all but slain, when with might and main
  He dealt forth an avenging blow:
Tell how the cry went up to the sky
  As chief by the chief was laid low.

*   *   *   *   *

O tale thrice told! Field of cloth of gold
  Was that field where the children played,
And the poppies' hue showed the crimson dew
  Which should fall with the evening shade:
Each flower they trod down, sprang back, a crown
  For the knight who was not afraid.

Little children, still your own sweet will
  Ye work in the fields of the world:
Yours the banner of youth, purity, truth,
  White and clear, for 'tis just unfurled,
And its fair device of Paradise
  By the laughing breeze is uncurled.

Why must the day of strife and dismay
  Come to you, with its blighting cares?
Why hasten to fight, each one a true knight,
  Whom the foe with the challenge dares,

While many a saint, heart-sick and faint,
  Is making for you sweetest prayers?

To hold your own? Nay, to win a throne
  As your righteous reward and due:
To keep house and land with your strong right hand,
  To be counted worthy and true;
To stand or fall at your Leader's call,
  To be faithful among the few.

Rank and name in the annals of fame,
  And a mark in history's page:
Shall these be your aim, and your highest claim,
  The honours and wealth of an age?
Not them, not them, 'tis the diadem
  That you seek for your heritage!

Ah! they wait to see your chivalry,
  Those Angels who sing in the Quire:
They are within, far away from the din
  Of the striving and fierce desire,
Lifting peaceful songs while earth's vast throngs
  Stand up in the thick of the fire.

What time they sing, the clarions ring,
   And the banners flash in the sky :
Hark! the Leader calls, and the evening falls ;
   The last dread assault must be nigh :
Soon the strife be done, coronal won,
   And the wreath that never shall die.

THE AGE OF WISDOM.

"O who will show us good?" they ask;
   "Say who will set us free,"
The beaten track, the weary task,
   Must these for ever be?

Why one dull round of weary days,
   Morning and noon and night,
Passed in set forms of prayer and praise,
   In looking for the light.

One way, a strange unaltered course,
   A mill-round for the soul:
Why cannot men take good by force—
   One action gain the goal?

The weary years at jog-trot pace
   Wear out the panting heart;
We are on fire, *will* win the race,
   Must seize the better part.

The times seem waxen slow again
  For men of eager mind ;
The age of chivalry must wane,
  When heroes lag behind.

There is no fighting to be done,
  No field whereon to try,
How fadeless laurels may be won,
  Or how a man can die.

More freedom, less of bond and ban,
  Freedom of will and thought :
No priestcraft for an upright man
  By self and nature taught."

Thus sighs the wisdom of to-day,
  Forgetting truth and right :
Fretful, impatient of delay,
  And stumbling in the night.

The age of heroes dawns once more,
  But fresh the battle-cry,
Alas ! the armour saints once wore
  Is out of date,—gone by.

Science and art but do their worst
　　When God is lightly feared ;
The strength of mind is strength accurst,
　　If against Heaven upreared.

Men doubt if God will intervene
　　When sickness taints the air :
Their Boards of Health, their red routine,
　　Are stronger far than prayer.

Pshaw! Judgment upon man and beast !
　　The world has grown too wise
On old-wives' theories to feast,
　　To meditate on lies.

" How glibly prate those pious fools,
　　Who talk of sins made plain,
By plague on man and beast !—the schools
　　Are forms of babes again."

Well, be it so : at any rate
　　The babes shall win the day,
When worldly-wisdom's addled pate
　　Has ached itself away.

Men's well-wrought plans must stay the tide,
  Of evil that sets in :
Good Government and British pride
  The mastery shall win.

Be clean, drain well, and baffle death ;
  Yet Death is at the door,
And Caution, thwarted, holds her breath
  Until the plague is o'er.

O nineteenth century, how wise,
  . By all thy sons extolled !
Spoilt by thy vain philosophies,
  And science, falsely called.

When wilt thou learn that God is still
  What God was evermore,
And bend to Him thine iron will
  As ages did before ?

Then shalt thou be an Age of Gold,
  God's purpose in thee seen :
Fairer than fairest years of old,
  Of all the ages, Queen !

SUNRISE IN THE CITY.

ONE by one, the golden stars are paling,
    Softly breaks the morning light:
One by one, the rosy clouds come sailing
    Slowly in the eastern height.

One by one, the fresh green leaves are shaking
    In the fitful early breeze:
One by one, the little birds are waking
    In their nests among the trees.

One by one, upon the restless river
    Flowing through the silent town,
Flecked with light and shadow, changing ever,
    Mimic waves dance up and down.

One by one, the smoke-clouds are outpouring
    Darkness into God's fair sky;
Wreath by wreath of blackness grimly soaring
    To the painted clouds on high.

One by one, the poor, the sick, the weary,
　Hail the blessed new-born day:
Hour by hour their vigil has been dreary,
　Now, thank God, 'tis passed away.

One by one, some distant sounds give warning
　Of fresh waking unto life:
Pray for those, who in the quiet morning,
　Struggle in the last dread strife.

EVENING LIGHT.

Soon must the sunlight die away,
  And shadows come ;
Shine forth, ye glorious stars, that we may see
  The way to reach our home.

So shall no wandering steps of ours—
  Leaps in the dark,
Doom us most justly to a wretched fate,
  And make us miss our mark.

Shine forth, that haply we may catch
  E'en through our tears
Glimpses of Heaven, enough to stay the tide
  Of our unworthy fears.

Enough to win us back from earth,
  From self and sin,
From every passion-breath which fans to flame
  A quenchless fire within.

Light springs for all the true of heart,
 And only they
Shall see unveiled, when golden stars fade out,
 The pure and perfect Day.

HID TREASURE.

WORLD, rich and selfish, call me poor,
   And treat me with your cold disdain :
Hard words the hardy can endure,
   Your taunts, your scorning are in vain.

Sun, moon, and stars, shine out for me,
   Earth lays her bounty at my feet ;
Each morn new forms of grace I see,
   Each night fresh mysteries I greet.

Out of the depths come voices dread,
   Which tell of things thou canst not learn :
And angels' wings around me spread,
   To something more than thee I turn.

All the great Past to me is wealth,
   A mine of buried thought and speech :
With muffled footsteps, as by stealth,
   Back to the awful dead I reach.

The Present with its meed of gold,
  Who robs me of my own to-day?
The Future with its vast untold,
  Who takes this heritage away?

O foolish world, how poor art thou,
  Love only gains the better part:
While thou dost crown ambition's brow,
  Thou canst not soothe one aching heart.

EVENING.

Now homeward go the kine with lowings sweet;
  The bird will soon be quiet in her nest:
The hills are with a tender glory drest
  By him who them at morn did bravely greet.
The western clouds seem like a golden fleet,
  Which for some happier land is setting sail,
  Making the peeping stars so meek and pale;
The silver lake lies quiet at our feet;
  The night breeze moans along with gentle wail,
  And softly stirs the blossom on the tree.
Light, fairy things to mossy beds do creep,
  As purple mists rise slowly o'er the vale;
The curfew peals across the fragrant lea,
  Chiming To-day, good gift of God, to sleep!

A SONG OF THE FIRST CHRISTMAS NIGHT.

THERE was silence in Bethlehem's fields that night,
  Where the shepherds their flocks were keeping ;
The stars calmly shone from their beautiful height,
  The sheep on the hills lay a-sleeping,
And the quiet that fell on that wondrous hour
  From all other was strangely parted,
And hope, that for years had been robb'd of her
    power,
  Was the hope of the weary-hearted.

How dreary the ages of strife passed away,
  Since word of His Coming was spoken !
Still, still the deep darkness that reigns ere the day,
  And quietness almost unbroken.
Through darkness and silence Peace hasted to earth,
  Where sheep on the hills lay a-sleeping,
And the Angel declared the wonderful Birth—
  The end of our sorrow and weeping.

Then suddenly came to this Angel most bright
   A host of the Heavenly Chorus,
And a glory brake forth more dazzling to sight
   Than the sun which at noon-day burns o'er us ;
The silence was over, the hope long deferred,
   The waiting for Christ and His glory,
When the Angels sang out, and the listeners heard
   The tidings they brought in their story.

THE MARTYRS OF THE UNIVERSITIES
MISSION, 1862.

OUR Mother lifts her voice on high;
   She sings to God with joyful calm;
Two sons of hers have fought the fight—
   Two heroes won the fadeless palm.

The Holy Ghost, the Paraclete,
   Has canonized these saints of ours,
Nor care we though the world may scorn,
   And taunt the Church with wasted powers.

O blessed work of Learning's homes,
   To offer first-fruits such as these;
A radiance from their classic halls
   Lights up the thrones of martyr-sees.

Thrice happy change! For Afric's toil
   The rest which Christ vouchsafes His own;
No feverish heats, or chilling waves,
   No wandering mind or altered tone.

And while o'er these fresh graves we mourn,
    Far sadder tears than ours are shed,
By those who sought to share the work,
    And found the husband—brother—dead.

Still it is thus that faith must strive,
    Though tears and loss her toils betide;
The pioneers, indeed, are fallen—
    The pastoral staff is laid aside.

Yet seed like this *must* bear its fruit;
    Was ever garner'd golden grain
Which danced in sunshine morn and eve,
    And knew not some dark days of rain?

OUTER WORSHIPPERS.

THERE are, who in some vast Cathedral nave
   Seek a brief respite from the city's din ;
We, too, but worship in the outer courts,
   And may not go the mystic shrine within.

Like them, we hear at best but broken notes
   Of alleluias, which are clear and strong :
We strain our eager eyes, and only catch
   Bright fleeting glimpses of the white-robed
      throng.

We may not gain that holiest place of all,
   Not yet our feet may tread its jewelled way ;
Nor are our voices tuned to swell those songs
   Which wreathe its ageless pillars day by day.

We look through that dim screen which bars us
   out—
   We think how blest they are who tarry there,
And then we seek the busy world afresh,
   Nerved for our duty by the vision fair.

'Tis but a little while we have to wait;
  Only until our work on earth be fully done
E'en now, the Lord within the golden gates
  His faithful souls is gathering, one by one.

Let us have faith ; we work and wait for God :
  Soon shall our life's hard day of toil be o'er,
And when, at eventide, the lamps are lit,
  We shall go in and worship evermore.

LITTLE WILLIE.

THE wind is blowing roughly
　　Against my window pane;
And, like a knell's sad tolling,
　　Drop, drop the drops of rain.
A dark and dreary evening,
　　Meet for a heart alone—
A heart which once had treasure
　　To clasp, and call its own!

I know·they took him from me,
　　And bore him far away;
I cannot but remember
　　That dark and bitter day.
Dead as he was I nursed him,
　　And held him to my breast;
Until, with words of comfort,
　　They laid my boy to rest.

And yet, somehow, I call him
　　As though he still would come
Back to his vacant corner—
　　Back from his narrow home.
'Willie!' I cry; '*my* Willie!'
　　But oh! I cry in vain;
Echoes fly back and mock me,
　　But *he* comes not again.

And then I see good angels
　　Shine forth from out the dark—
Like lights upon the ocean
　　Lest men should miss their mark.
And low, mysterious murmurs
　　Swell in the twilight dim,
'He shall not come for ever,
　　But thou shalt go to him!'

HARVEST HOME CAROL.

NIGHT as clear as day,
   Save that refulgent noon,
Gives place to silver ray,
   Shed from the full orb'd moon ;
Outlines sharp and clear,
   And, wrapped in pallid sheen,
The landscape far and near,
   By Cynthia, gracious queen.

Golden fields o'erswept
   By sickles keen and bright,
The Harvest-home is kept
   For all is stored to-night :
Garnered safe the wheat,
   And sure the poor man's bread :
Sheep, oxen in our street,
   And plenteous tables spread.

Famine, pale and gaunt,
  Faint Hunger with its sting,
And fever-fires that haunt,
  And want and woe take wing;
Spread the board of God,
  The poor are satisfied,
To Him be thanks and laud,
  His Name be magnified.

ON FINDING THE NAVE OF WELLS CATHEDRAL STREWN WITH LEAVES.

SAID the leaves, "We have dwelt the whole sum-
    mer long,
Beneath the shade of this House of Song ;
We have heard such beautiful strains soar on high,
We long to hear more before we die,—
To be sung to our rest, with the notes divine
Which swell for aye, from that ancient shrine."

The glorious days of the summer flew by,
The time was come when the leaves must die ;
And the autumn breeze, through the half-opened
    door
Bare them in love to S. Andrew's floor,
Where, at sundown, when evensong had been said,
Chanted to rest, they lay scattered and dead !

THE DEATH-CRY.

THEY tell us when an ill-starr'd ship*
Was going down, from every lip
A cheer brake forth which rent the air,
Cry of the brave in wild despair.
But surely when the cheer was past,
There came a moment's prayer at last ;
A cry for mercy, ere the sea
Engulphed them all so cruelly :
Words which, perchance, too long passed o'er,
A mother's love had taught of yore.

* H.M.S. *Orpheus.*

THE MOTHERLESS BABE AT SEA AT CHRISTMAS-TIDE.

THROUGH whistling wind, o'er crested wave,
Proud ship, bear on to me the child,
The little babe whose presence mild
A father's heart must fondly crave.

Yet he must mourn, and mourn alone,
Thy mother gone to rest, and thee,
Tossing upon the stormy sea :
Both torn away, both still his own.

Ah ! friends, how bitter 'tis that tears
Spring to the eyes on Christmas morn,
When all the world sings, " Christ is born,"
But sorrows thicken with the years.

Where is thy mother, little one ?
Where is she gone who carried thee
Forth from her home, far o'er the sea, ·
To leave thee when the voyage was done ?

Dear little babe, I tell thee where;
She hears the blessed Angels sing
Around the cradle of their King,
She watches all the Mother's care.

She sees the little children play,
Peep in and out, as half afraid
To gaze where God the Word is laid,
Then thinks of you, so far away.

" O Mary, let me watch beside
The new-born Child, whilst thou shalt bear
(Great Mother, wonderful and fair)
My babe to me from yon dark tide."

Then in her ears the joy-bells play
As Mary soothes the moment's pain :
" Wife, husband, child shall meet again,
And keep in Heaven their Christmas Day."

Ring on sweet bells ! the Christ-Child wins,
For mother and the babe she nursed :
And Death, my friends, is best, not worst,
When earth fades out and Heaven begins.

AT NIGHT IN ILLNESS.

In my sick room
The angels come and go;
A pure, unearthly glow
   Lights up its gloom,
Some of that shining throng
Come to keep vigil all night long.

   And faces bright
Are crowding round my bed—
The peaceful, blessed dead
   Arrayed in light—
Friends loved in years past o'er,
Come back to smile on me once more.

   Flowers near me lie
Which dear ones brought to-day;
I watch them fade away,
   And gently die;—
Which shall be first to fall
He only knows, Who knoweth all.

To me, sometimes,
Mysterious whispers come :
Voices which call me home—
    Like distant chimes
Heard when, all wanderings past,
One nears the heart's true rest at last.

And more than this—
Songs in the night I gain :
Full many an angel strain
    Of holy bliss ;—
Sent to prepare my ear
For melodies more sweet and clear.

I will not pray
For treasures once held dear :
Now, things seen very near,
    Once far away;
Each hour shows something new,
The False fades out and all is True.

*   *   *   *   *

Lord, when we die,
Send forth Thine angels sweet
To bear us to Thy Feet,
  That there we lie
Until the shadows flee,
And all Thy saints rejoice with Thee !

SAINT RAPHAEL, ARCHANGEL.

Saint most gentle, fair Archangel,
   Dost thou really love me?
Dost thou shield me, sweetly spreading
   Shelt'ring wings above me?
Beauteous in thy pure estate,
Princely and Inviolate!

Yes, I know it, lord of cohorts,
   Thou dost deign to guide me;
In my going, in my coming,
   Thou from ill dost hide me,
Shaping all my footsteps well,
Glorious Saint Raphael!

Thou, with stainless hands for ever,
   Prayers of saints presentest,
Serving always, tiring never,
   For thy will assentest
To His perfect Will, Who owns
Virtues, Powers, Dominions, Thrones!

From the sunshine and the glory
   Round the Throne eternal,
Like a dust speck thou dost see me,
   Thou in Light supernal,
I, so far, so far away,
Struggling o'er the Narrow Way.

Ah ! dear Angel, thou dost sorrow
   When by sins I grieve thee :
When I falter, grow impatient,
   Thou dost seem to leave me ;
What if then thy hands upbear,
Said for me, some saintly prayer ?

When death's shades are o'er me stealing
   In their wondrous fashion ;
Then, sweet guide, for me be pleading
   Jesu's bitter Passion :
He, thy Monarch, give command,
" Raphael, bear him in thy hand !"

A CAROL.

CHRISTIANS, carol sweetly,
   Up, to-day, and sing!
'Tis the happy birthday
   Of our Holy King :
Haste we then to greet Him,
   Humbly falling down,
While our hands entwine Him,
   Dearest Babe, a crown!

Crowds of snow-white angels
   Throng the golden stair ;
All things are delightful,
   All things passing fair :
Bells, clear music making,
   Peal the news to earth ;
Chimes within, make answer,
   All is glee and mirth.

Michael, at the manger,
  Bows his royal face ;
Gabriel, with lily,
  Hides transcendent grace :
For, dear friends, the glory
  Of that lowly bed
Overpowers the beauty
  On Archangels shed.

Shall I tell of Joseph,
  Who, with rapt surprise,
Sees the light of Godhead
  Fill those infant eyes ?
Shall I sing of Mary,
  Who, upon her breast,
Cradles her Creator,
  Soothes Him to His rest ?

Angels, Mary, Joseph,
  Yes ! I greet you all !
Falling down in worship
  At the manger stall !

A Carol.

For you hail our Monarch,
Born a Child to-day :
So, with you I worship,
And my homage pay.

PROCESSIONAL LITANY.

LORD of Hosts, to Thee we cry,
Cross and banner raise on high ;
In our time of need draw nigh ;
> Hear us, Holy Trinity.

From the foes who seek to ban,
From the subtle craft of man,
Keep us, for none other can ;
> Hear us, Holy Jesu.

By Thy Presence with the Bride,
By Thy Wounds, now glorified,
Guard, whatever ills betide ;
> Hear us, Holy Jesu.

Foes without and fears within,
Arm of flesh and ranks of sin,
Christ, o'er these the triumph win ;
> Hear us, Holy Jesu.

Nerve the hands which bear the sword,
Break the serried, hostile horde ;
Thy dear peace on all be poured ;
> Hear us, Holy Jesu.

When the strife of tongues is heard
In the House of God the Word,
When its calm by storms is stirred ;
> Hear us, Holy Jesu.

Rent and tearful East and West,
Zion spreads her hands distrest ;
Master give Thy people rest ;
> Hear us, Holy Jesu.

Grant us peace, but if the fight
Thickens with the falling night,
All the Saints defend the right !
> Hear us, Holy Jesu.

Then at last shall come the Day,
Triumph crown the life-long fray ;
Lord, till then, we work and pray,
> Help us, Holy Jesu.

MARTHA AND MARY.

IN MEMORIAM, S. RAPHAEL'S, OCT. 19TH, 1870.

RICH and poor together meet
Low before the Master's Feet:
Young and old, yet Christ to them
Grants the self-same Requiem.

Mary chose the better part,
Martha served with all her heart;
Love and service lay them down,
Waiting full Reward and Crown.

Thus the Master, young and old
Gathers to His peaceful Fold;
He the Lamb of God confest,
Grant them His eternal Rest.

"RITUALISM."

A DOOR is open'd in Heaven to-day, and I get me
    a vision all fair,
A throne with the Lamb in the midst is seen, in His
    beauty beyond compare,
And a sea of glass, and a rainbow arch, and a throng
    in vestments of white,
Who prostrate fall and their *Sanctus* lift where the
    seven lamps of Fire shed their light.

"What!" cries the World, "do you really think
    that the glory of Heaven is like this?
"O fools, to believe that worship and song will fill
    up your measure of bliss:
"Better gifts I bestow, the love of the world, am-
    bition's reward and renown."
O World, thy rewards will be wanting *there*, thy
    pomp, and thy perishing crown.

See! Angel-borne censers are flinging the smoke
    of incense up to the Throne,
Powers, Principalities veiling their face from glories
    to mortals unknown ;
And the City four-square, rings forth with the shout,
    "Worthy the Lamb that was slain."
The City of peace, where, tears wip'd away, there
    is no more sorrow or pain.

"What !" rails the Flesh, "do you really think that
    the joy of your Heaven will be found
" In vestments and lights, prostrations and forms,
    and prayers in a wearisome round ?
" I have better delights than these for mine, pride
    of life, and lust of the eyes."
O Flesh, pride and lust will have no place *there*, nor
    the serpent in angel's guise.

Her gates are of pearl, and her city gold, her foun-
    dations of precious stone,
Nor ray of the sun, nor of silver moon for light in
    her borders is shown ;

And the cry goes up like the thunder's peal, or the
    sound of the waters' force,
As the nine-fold ranks of the Angel-choir, sweetest
    antiphons sing in course.

"What!" sneers the Fiend, "Do you really think
    that your Heaven is a temple of praise,
"Where Intellect falls at visions of God, through
    ages of infinite days?
"Man worship thyself, thou, greater than He, be
    throned in a temple as well."
O Fiend, thy dark form is never seen *there*, nor one
    of thy legions of hell.

Ah! the World, I suppose, is worldly wise, and
    the Flesh to the flesh is true,
And the Devil stands well to the gates of Hell,
    lest his victims grow too few;
Foolish and weak, superstitious, misled; thus
    these three in their pride condemn,
But I turn me once more to the open door of the
    New Jerusalem.

PERSEVERANCE.

My heart henceforth is Thine, dear Lord, not mine,
   In it I pray Thy will, not mine, be done ;
My life, myself to Thee I now resign,
   Ah! happy soul if now thy race wert run !

I want the crown of life, I want the prize,
   And casting self and selfishness away,
I want henceforth to fear no foe's surprise,
   Since Grace Divine lights up my heart this day.

I want, just now, to see the golden shore,
   I want, just now, in Thee to feel secure ;
Once far from home, I want to stray no more,
   Once vile, I want to be for ever pure.

And yet for more than three and thirty years
   Thou waitedst, Who this weary world couldst save
Without a life of agony and tears,
   Without the Cross, the Passion, or the Grave.

Within the Virgin's Womb, at Nazareth,
  Beneath the olives of Gethsemane,
Thy patient waiting sought in life, in death,
  Then I must wait, O patient Love, for Thee.

Thus by restraint must I too win the goal,
  Grow perfect as the end of all grows near :
This, Lord, vouchsafe to give my eager soul,
  Repose in Thee, and grace to persevere.

SINS OF THE TONGUE.

In days gone past, a monk, they say,
  With angry words a brother stung,
Not thinking of the price to pay
  For speaking with a thoughtless tongue.

That very night the brother died,
  Whose soul a comrade's words had vex'd ;
Thus many pass away to hide
  This world's unkindness in the next.

And while the monk in sorrow bent,
  Thinking of words beyond recall,
An Angel to his cell was sent,
  To question for the Lord of All.

" Your brother lies in yonder cell,
  Last night your anger guaged his crime ;
Say, shall I bear to Heaven or Hell
  The soul you judged before its time ?"

The monk fell down, ashamed, afraid,
  Was *he* the judge, to bless or doom?
Thus doubly bitter tears are made,
  Shed o'er an injured brother's tomb.

HEAVEN.

O HAPPY halls of light,
   We sing your grace to-day,
Your glories, passing bright,
   Which never fade away.

O happy souls that win
   Your joy and perfect peace,
Set free from bonds of sin,
   In you they find release.

The saints you show at length,
   The bands of soldiers true,
Made strong in Jesu's strength
   To suffer and to do.

And, fair surpassing thought,
   In robe of golden sheen,
With divers colours wrought,
   The virgins' spotless Queen.

And, sight to gladden more
 Than all the rest beside :
He Whom the saints adore,
 The Lamb of God Who died.

And you are far away,
 And you are hard to win,
My Home of fadeless day,
 My Rest from strife with sin ?

Yet One beside me stands
 Who never fails His own,
But bears them in His Hands,
 And guides them to His throne.

Ah! if I *will* be crowned,
 And if I *will* be true :
A heaven on earth is found
 To brighten into you.

THE SUMMER SNOW.

My little maid, but just turned three,
Spake sweetly thus one day to me :
" How is it in the spring-time's glow,
The grass is white with flakes of snow ?

For when I went to bed last night,
Dear father, all the lawn was bright
With daisy's eyes amongst the green ;
Now neither grass nor flower is seen."

" Dear little one, who all would know,
This is God's gentle summer snow ;
The shower of fragrant blossom leaves,
Which earth to her warm breast receives.

While you last night slept safe and sound,
A gentle zephyr strewed the ground
With all those pearly blooms that made,
For humming bees a fragrant shade."

Ah! little girl, if winter lower
For you in happy sunlight hour,
Think of the grass and flowers below ;
God hides them with His summer snow.

A· PAINTER'S LEGEND.

A PAINTER, long ago, wrought out the story
  Of the great love of Christ our Lord ;
How He the Prince of Life and Glory,
  The Very and Eternal Word,
Enthroned before the glassy sea,
Still mourns for sin exceedingly.

And thus he pictured Him Whose look so tender
  No art may paint, no hues express :
God in His majesty of splendour,
  But wearing still His Passion-dress—
The purple robe which may not hide
His wounded Hands and Feet and Side.

Once more His blessed Face looks marred with
    anguish ;
  His Brow still bears the thorny crown,
And still in death He seems to languish,
  And in an agony look down
On those who nail Him yet again
Fast to the Cross of sharpest pain.

THE BISHOP AND THE WIDOW.

NOT so very long ago in a dim cathedral aisle,
A Bishop knelt, his office said, to pray a little while;
He prayed so long and prayed so well he fell into
    a trance,
And a widow knelt beside him as we should say
    by chance.

The Bishop watched the widow's tears drop slowly
    one by one,
And as he gazed an angel came in brightness like
    the sun;
Who stored within a casket rare each tear-drop as
    it fell,
"Surely, my God," the prelate said, "that widow
    prayeth well."

"Tell me, good woman, what you ask, what grace
    you seek to gain,
"Since God sends forth a messenger to store each
    tear and pain;

" Some special favour from His Hand you surely
ask to-day,

" Some sweet devotion to the Saints, or vow to
Jesus pay."

" My lord," the widow trembling said, " I do but
say the prayers

" That year by year have soothed my heart and
lightened all my cares ;

" The *Creed* and the *Our Father ;* my lord, from out
the heart

" I say my simple prayers and know that God will
do His part."

Learn to be real, this will bring good Angels to
your side,

Who to the throne of God will bear the tears you
fain would hide ;

Nor ask of Him some mighty gifts, or wondrous
thing to do :

He heard the widow's prayers because her heart
within was true.

THE HOLY INNOCENTS.

RACHEL weeping for her children,
  Flowers in early spring laid low;
None may comfort, none may cheer her,
  Faint and pallid, full of woe.
Yet the slain are girt with triumph,
  They shall swell the victor's song;
Theirs the crown with scarce a struggle,
  First-fruits of the martyr-throng.

Bethlehem's streets are dark with mourning,
  All is woe and wild despair;
But within the Heavenly City
  John beholds a vision fair:
Little ones with palms rejoicing
  In their happy, high estate,
Following with eager footsteps,
  Christ, the Lamb Immaculate.

There, in that Eternal Country,
　Men of peace have peace for aye ;
There the sword is sheathed for ever,
　Foes are banished far away.
Here, Lord, mortify within us
　Vices which Thine Eye offend :
Keep us, children, pure and holy,
　Constant, faithful, to the end.　Amen.

PASSION SUNDAY.

SOUNDS of strife are heard to-day,
Trumpets calling to the fray :
Thunder over Zion breaks,
As the strife of tongues awakes.
Desolation, woe and doom
Hasten on in awful gloom,
All is tumult, wild unrest,
Where the God of Peace hath blest.

Israel, art thou first to smite,—
First to do thy Lord despite ?
He shall speak, and stone by stone
Of the temple fall, o'erthrown.
Prophets came to thee in vain,
Proudly thou didst all disdain,
Vain the years of trial lent,
Now thy children stone the Sent.

Who shall conquer in the strife,
Light or Darkness, Death or Life?
Which lie vanquished on the field,
Which in shame and anguish yield?
When the fight its course has run,
When the victory is won,
Whose the banner, which shall tell
How his foeman, smitten, fell?

What if hell her legions bring?
Thou shalt triumph glorious King:
What if earth shall nail Thee fast
Till the dread Three Hours are past?
From the Cross, Thy Manhood's throne,
Thou shalt battle for Thine own,
Gain the Mastery of Love,
Win the constant crowns above.

When our Passion-tide is o'er,
Breaks the Easter-Evermore:
May we see Thee, gracious Lord,
Taste the joys of Thy Reward:

Alleluias sweet outpour,
Thee, our Lord, our Love adore,
All Redemption's work complete,
Every foe beneath Thy Feet.

Forward then with Christ to-day,
See, His banner leads the way!
Forward, brave the fire and flood,
Sing the Cross and Precious Blood.
Praise the Lord of Life and Death,
Praise Him everything with breath,
Praise Him, Saints, ye Stars and Light,
Praise Him, Angels in the height!   Amen.

THE CIRCUMCISION.

INFANT Jesus, we adore Thee,
　　Come the Law's demand to pay ;
Cross and Passion lie before Thee,
　　And Thy Sacred Blood to-day
Flows, that sinners may implore Thee
　　In the bloodless Rite for aye.

Seven days angels have been singing
　　Songs more sweet as each has run ;
On the eighth, we hear them bringing,
　　(Number of perfection won),
Yet one more, an octave ringing
　　To the praise of God the Son.

Yes ! they hail the blessed flowing
　　Of the Precious Blood of God,
Which hereafter, brightly glowing,
　　Speaking " better things " abroad,
Shall to all the world be showing
　　Cause for never ending laud.

Louder than at first creation,
    Lift they now their songs to greet
Blood, the price of earth's salvation,
    Shed for man in drops most sweet,
· Crimson tide of expiation,
    For the world's transgression meet.

Worthy is the Lamb of blessing,
    Worship, honour, laud, and might!
Who are these, His Name confessing
    In the fire and in the fight?
Who shall be His love expressing
    In the well-won halls of light?

They who through much tribulation
    Wage the war and bear the Rood:
They who shall have won salvation,
    Stormed the gate and crossed the flood.
Sing, to-day, with exultation
    Shedding of the Precious Blood!

THE SAINTS AND THE WORLD.

POOR world, poor world, what would'st thou be,
Without the saints to pray for thee ?
Without their love to intercede,
Without their heavenly grace to plead,
Without their strength to hold thee up,
Their sorrows in thy brimming cup ?

Thou know'st it not, but these are thine
By many a token, many a sign ;
We see the mark of saintly hands
Where scoffing irreligion stands,
And cruel pride and wild despite,
Unwilling, catch some borrow'd light.

For, as the sun on noisome place
Pours down his flood of beauteous grace,
So saints, upon a world of woe,
Shed gleams which sometimes gild it so,
That often, to the outward gaze,
It glitters fair in heavenly rays.

But to the eye which looks within,
There breaks a glimpse of woe and sin ;
The saints are Christ's, the world its own ;
They serve, it lives for self alone ;
The saints are poor, the world is great,
The saints are love, the world is hate.

Still world, poor world, what would'st thou be,
Without the saints to pray for thee ?
Who knows the vengeance and the hurt
Which daily orisons avert ?
Who tells the judgments turned away,
Because a saint of God can pray ?

All Saints !   O wondrous power is yours
Which hatred of the world endures :
More wondrous still, the love of One
Who to your starry host is Sun,
The King of Saints, Who all day stands,
To sinners stretching forth His Hands.

JESUS AND HIS CHILD.

STRIVING, struggling, falling,
    Battling with the foe ;
This, the life-long trial
    In the march below :
But the Voice of Jesus,
    Comes to calm my fear :
" I will not forsake thee,
    Trust Me, I am near."

Sinful, weak, distrustful,
    Striving self to please ;
Choosing always smooth things,
    Loving sloth and ease :
" Up !" the Voice is crying,
    " Bear with Me the Cross,
Turn aside from pleasure,
    Dare to suffer loss."

Weary, heavy-laden,
　Sad with weight of sin?
How shall I, so guilty,
　Love of Jesus win?
" How shall Jesus love thee,
　Child, what dost thou say?
Have not I redeemed thee?
　Canst thou turn away?

Tell Me; sin's forgiveness,
　Dost thou this believe?
Wilt thou spurn Me from thee?
　Or My grace receive?
Child make answer quickly,
　' I Thy love would know,
And, until Thou bless me,
　Will not let Thee go.' "

Master, I believe Thee,
　Lo! the cleansing flood
In Thy Church is flowing,
　'Tis the Precious Blood:

O, the Voice of pardon
  Breathed in words divine!
Jesus, Lord and Master,
  Be that pardon mine.

PRAYERS FOR THE DEAD.

DEEPER and deeper grew the shadows, till at last,
To mortal eyes, thick night set in and all was past.

All love could do was done, all hope seemed
    driven away,
Then faith lit up her torch and bade the mourners
    pray.

So life and death are one, locked in one sweet em-
    brace,
For ever growing, deepening in the world of grace.

So love burns brighter, though to time and sense,
The scarcely dead, so well remembered, are gone
    hence.

"Safe home," within the Paradise of God they
    dwell
Wrapped round about with light and peace
    ineffable.

Ineffable and yet not perfect; *that* the Christ
Wills to be wrought, through Him, by prayer and
    Eucharist.

Then I may pray for all the faithful dead: I ask
Rest for their souls; at once love's sharpest, sweet-
    est task. .

Full consummation; yes, the fulness Thou canst
    give
To those who in the mystery of death still live.

And Thou rebuk'st me not, Thou Who Thyself
    wast laid,
Dead, with the grave-clothes round Thee, in the
    tomb's dark shade.

All things depart; hot fever-change smites east
    and west,
Unchanging still the prayer—"Grant them eternal
    rest!"

Undying, quenchless, strong, great God of quick
    and dead,
Till in the morning light all things are perfected.

ON SEEING AN OLD WOMAN TELLING HER BEADS IN CHEAPSIDE.

POOR old woman, no doubt the world thinks you a
wretched fanatic
To trouble yourself with your beads and your
prayers in the street ;
You had far better do your devotions at home, in
your attic :
It gives it such pain to regard you as dust at its
feet.

You are too superstitious, the world, you know,
hates superstition ;
It loves moderation and soberness, even in prayer;
Be religious, oh, certainly if it improves your po-
sition,
Be respectable, yes, but all its devotion ends
there.

But perchance, as you're poor, the kind world will
    accord you permission
  To break through its rules, and say prayers
    to your God in its face:
It allows for the foibles of people of tenth-rate
    condition,
  Those whom it has spurned, may, perhaps, need
    a little more grace.

Poor old woman, the world, as you know, is un-
    commonly clever,
  And it tells you, you say all your prayers by
    rote and machine;
It has found out enigmas and solved hardest pro-
    blems, but never
  Discovered the deep things of faith, or pierced
    through the unseen.

You are wanting in intellect; this is no age for
    devotion,
  Pray don't show the world that you think of
    your soul or your prayers;

12

It dislikes our Lord's peace in the midst of its
  strife and commotion,
  What *has* Heaven to do with the barter of stocks
  and of shares ?

You know nothing of bank-books, of interest,
  great speculations,
  Of trade and its laws, of its maxims as pure
  as the snow :
You have treasure in Heaven, *there* at least you
  have great expectations,
  Unfit for society, now, poor old soul, you may
  go !

PROCESSIONAL FOR ASCENSION-TIDE.

To the Holy Hill of God we go,
   To His Tabernacle fair ;
We leave the world and its cares below,
   Borne on by the force of prayer :
And the ageless gates are thrown open wide,
That the King may pass with His chosen Bride.
                    Alleluia.

For before His people goes the Lord,
   From the wilderness of sin
He leads His own to their great reward,
   The eternal Halls to win :
And He scatters Kings in the trembling world,
And the foes of His Face are downward hurled.
                    Alleluia.

In the Holy Place His strength is shown,
  In the Sanctuary's shade :
Before the grace of Calvary's Throne,
  Mount Sinai melts, afraid :
And the saintly host wondrous spoil divides,
Where the Lord of Hosts His prowess hides.
                    Alleluia.

To the Holy Hill of God we go,
  To His Tabernacle fair ;
And brighter far than Mount Tabor's glow,
  It shines, for our God is there :
And we hail His Wounds in their crimson stain,
For He will not leave His elect again.
                    Alleluia.

Alleluias lift, fair Angel-Quire,
  Your King is crowned to-day,
And we to join in those songs aspire,
  Which cheer us along our way.
Then let earth be glad, and let Heaven adore,
For the Lord hath triumphed for evermore.
                    Alleluia.

ONE LORD—ONE FAITH.

Is it in vain we pray for peace,
   While signs and notes of strife abound,
In vain we ask that war may cease,
   While hostile forces camp around?

Rough billows, waters wild and dread,
   Still bear the Ark upon their breast,
But God's fair rainbow over head,
   Is sign of peace and pledge of rest.

Say, will the wingèd prayers we send
   Forth from the Ark, return again?
Yes, some have come to point the end,
   To tell of sunshine after rain.

They bear the olive-branch to show
   That flood and storm are passing o'er;
Our hearts are strong, for well we know
   The waters shall o'erwhelm no more.

What if through patient prayer we reap
　　But taunt and gibe and angry din?
The shrieking wind, the surging deep,
　　These are without, but Peace within.

The world may scorn, the jester sneer,
　　But prayer than hate is stronger still;
Daily the cry, each day more dear,
　　"Such peace alone as is Thy Will."

Thy Will, dear Lord, Whose parting prayer
　　Was unity for thine elect;
The East, the West, Thy promise share,
　　Blessing of peace from Thee expect.

Safe from the strife of tongues, O God,
　　Within Thy Tabernacle hide
The sheep, who, scattered far abroad,
　　Spurn the Good Shepherd as their Guide.

What can the force of prayer resist?
　　Father, Thy Will on earth be done:
One Altar serve for Eucharist,
　　And East and West in Thee be One.

TO THE HOLY CHURCH.

HAIL, Bride of God the Spirit,
　　Hail, Mother undefiled,
Hail, Virgin highly favoured,
　　Unsullied, unbeguiled,
Hail, Shrine indwelt, for sinners,
　　By Mary's holy Child !

The storm and tempest heighten,
　　The strife of tongues is heard ;
All these without—within thee,
　　The Peace of God the Word,
Felt nearest as the foemen
　, With sword and buckler gird.

O Mother, crowned with sorrows,
　　The sorrows of the King,
The cruel sword shall pierce thee,
　　And woes thy spirit wring ;
But after these, the triumph
　　Of Jesus thou shalt sing.

Beneath the olive's shadows
   The lily fairer grew :
When night was at its darkest
   The dawning struggled through :
Till breaks Redemption's morning,
   Be patient, suffer, do!

The wondrous salutation
   Of Gabriel still falls
Fresh from the Throne, the Presence,
   The everlasting Halls :
Fear not, O highly Favoured,
   Though foes besiege thy walls.

Fear not, the Lord is with thee,
   Elect, Inviolate ;
The Palace He hath chosen
   Of virginal estate!
Henceforth, all generations
   Shall call thee blessed, great !

THE CALL OF CHRIST.

"ALL the day long I stretch my Hands
While Israel gainsays and rejects :
In blindness still her King expects,
While at her gates her Saviour stands.

All the day long upon the tree
My Arms for her I open wide,
Show wounds in Hands, and Feet, and Side,
And call her, saying, Look and see !

Was ever love such love as Mine ?
What more could have been done for thee
Than I have done ; O answer Me,
And yet my people give no sign."

Thus still the Master's Voice is heard
Whenever Saint rebuking cries :
"Your Lord is here Whom ye despise,
The very and eternal Word !"

Acknowledge Him, His Cross accept,
And shape your own by bearing His,
Be friends of Christ, not enemies,
By gusts of hostile passions swept.

And follow Him Who calls to-day;
Leave all behind, press forward now;
As slave unto a master bow,
And choose to tread the narrow way.

You cast your nets deep down in sea,
You toil to earn the daily bread,
Yet you must cease if this be said,
Leave all, and come and follow Me.

O happy they who heed the call,
Leave ship, or house, or land for One
Who from the shore each faithful son
Bids come to Him, forsaking all!

FESTIVALS OF ASSOCIATIONS OF WOMEN.

THOU Who didst own a Mother's love,
Regard us from Thy Throne above,
We come to Thee in lowliness,
Thy servants' work vouchsafe to bless.

We raise the fallen, cheer the faint,
But Thou alone canst mould the Saint :
Where most we fail, Thou winnest most,
Assist us with Thy Holy Ghost.

We go to cheer the Magdalene,
To show her we with Thee have been ;
And all Thy words of mercy tell
Within the very gates of hell.

The little ones, Thy lambs, we feed,
And bear them in their hour of need ;
Warn those who tread the paths of sin,
And all the unbaptized bring in.

And as along the King's Highway,
We watch for souls from day to day,
We seek from street or court, some gem
To deck our Monarch's Diadem.

What if the world, in hurrying by,
Deride, or cast a scornful eye ?
Wert Thou esteemed of men, dear Lord,
Or is the Cross no more abhorred ?

Like Martha we will serve Thee still,
Like Mary sit and learn Thy Will :
And with all holy women gain
Our crown through strife, contempt, and pain.

Own us with those gone on before,
Who taught the self-same Faith of yore ;
And give us in our Home to see
The fruit of labours wrought in Thee.

Amen.

CAROL OF THE ANNUNCIATION.

ST. GABRIEL came to Mary,
  And greeting thus spake he :
" Hail ! thou so highly favoured,
  The Lord is now with thee."
Lady, of such sweet grace possest,
Among all women thou art blest.

But when Saint Mary saw him,
  And his saluting heard,
Her lowly soul was troubled :
  She marvelled at his word.
Lady and Maid, once sore distrest,
All generations call thee blest.

Thus said the fair Archangel,
  " Mary, fear not, for Thou
With God hast found full favour,
  Though trouble takes thee now."
Lady, our Lord shall seek thy breast,
Among all women thou art blest.

" Thou shalt conceive, pure Maiden,
    And bringing forth a Son,
Shalt call Him, Jesus, Saviour
    Of those by sin undone."
Lady, the Mother-maid confest,
All generations call thee blest.

" To Him shall God deliver
    His father David's throne,
And He shall reign for ever,
    His power be ne'er o'erthrown."
Lady, this King shall be thy guest,
Among all women thou art blest.

Then spake the Ever-Virgin,
    " My lord, how shall this be ?
But even as thou sayest,
    So be it unto me."
Lady, thy Son brings Joy and Rest,
Henceforth all nations call thee blest !

THE FORGIVENESS OF SINS.

WHAT can I do, dear Jesus,
  Since Thou hast all things done ?
Thy work for me completed,
  The victory is won :
If only sin be hated, .
  And penitence be shown,
My love in thee shall triumph,
  And thou my faith wilt own.

There is no condemnation
  Since Thou hast died for me :
No more a slave, in Jesus
  I stand for ever free :
If only in confession
  I own the power of God,
My sins are all forgiven,
  And scattered far abroad.

The Law's dread thunders dying,
  The Gospel's music rings,
And to the heart that wills it,
  Mount Calvary's sweetness brings :
If only I am faithful,
  And keep my Lord's commands,
No more the old handwriting
  Of ordinances stands.

I have no price for payment,
  For Thou hast justified ;
But heart and soul I give Thee,
  Cleansed, washed, and sanctified :
From first to last 'tis Jesus,
  Not self, but Thee, my Love ;
And Thee it is I offer,
  To God, enthroned above.

FROM SUNDAY TO SUNDAY.

I.—PALM SUNDAY.

BLESSED is He that cometh! I greet Thee, Master
    dear,
I cast myself before Thee, for the strife is drawing
    near;
And Thou wilt own the servant who hides himself
    in Thee,
From the tyranny and tempest, and the woe that
    is to be.

Blessed is He that cometh! 'Tis Thou dost an-
    swer make;
Blessed the faithful servant who the Master's Cross
    will take;
Who casts his sins before Me, that I may purge
    away
The stains of My redeemed one, with Love's con-
    suming ray.

Hosannah in the highest! the City of Peace is
    moved,
The heart goes forth in trembling to welcome her
    Beloved,
And as if she scarcely knew Him, asks, doubting,
    "Who is this?"
But the Son of David seeks her with the Eye that
    cannot miss.

O wondrous soul-procession that meets the Christ
    to-day!
But who of these will follow in the steep and
    rugged way,—
In the path of sorrows comfort, to Calvary
    ascend,
And wait throughout the Passion, and watch until
    the end?

The men who cry Hosannah, and lift the strain on
    high,
Shall they thrust nail and spear in, shall they shout
    Crucify?

O soul, look well within thee, lest thou the Lord
    betray,
Lest the King of Zion seek thee, and find thee
    turned away.

II.—THURSDAY IN HOLY WEEK.

The extremest anguish of the Passion nears,
    The guest-chamber is ready, and the hour is come,
When awful words break on the Apostles' ears,
    Words hard to understand, of mysteries the sum.

For Jesus gives His Body and His Blood,
    Himself the spotless Victim, as Himself the
        Priest;
O Manna blest, O precious, cleansing Flood,
    On this last night bestowed in Eucharistic Feast.

Thrice blessed Rite, wherein the Crucified
    Is evermore set forth to loving, faithful hearts;
Gift, in Whose strength the strong in faith abide,
    Peace, in Whose wondrous power the Christian
        soul departs.

III.—GOOD FRIDAY.

Faith looks with steadfast gaze
　To one, one only point, the Cross of Christ ;
Brightly it burns, though cloud or haze
　Shroud for awhile the Sign unpriced.

With reverent, folded hands,
　With eye to that one Centre always true,
Through storm and sunshine still she stands,
　Blest if she have but that in view.

For love of Him Who died,
　Love's Victim, on thy breast, O Royal Tree,
Nothing is sweet to her beside,
　Nothing is hers, O Cross, save thee !

IV.—EASTER EVEN.

Stars softly shine upon the tomb of God,
　The silent hours glide past ;
When will the Morning spread her wings abroad,
　The Sabbath be o'erpast ?

Chill night-airs, passing, kiss the shivering trees,
   Then die, as if afraid
To stir that quiet, e'en with gentlest breeze,
   Where the Dead Christ is laid.

The slumberous watch their faithless vigils keep,
   While Angels hover near,
Trembling to gaze upon that awful Sleep,
   The Rest from nail and spear.

How lately borne the scoffing and the shame !
   How yawned the Wounds Divine !
O Death, which gives the grave a fair, new name,
   Wounds, which are health to mine !

O precious Sleep, which, in its silent strength
   Masters the powers of night !
O Resurrection, which shall bring at length
   Immortal Life to Light !

V.—EASTER-DAY.

Sepulchred and wave-washed dead,
Sleepers where no mortal tread

Breaks the silence of your rest,
Deep in gorge, on mountain's crest;
There is news for you to-day,
Christ the King hath been your way,
In His beauty past compare,
Lord of life and Victor fair :
He Whose garment is the Light,
He Whose strong right Hand of might
Shattered hell and burst its bars,
Glorious in His wounds and scars :
Fresh from conflict with the foe,
Red in His apparel's glow,
Fresh from conquest won alone,
Won for ever for His own.

Through the city's gloom He went,
Where the living are content,
For the greed of gain, to sell
Bodies He redeemed so well :
Through the yards of nameless graves,
He Who the forgotten saves ;
Through the long cathedral aisle,
Where the fitful sunbeams smile,

As they seem in sport to pass
Through the many-tinted glass :
And He marked the sleepers there,
Priest and noble, young and fair,
And the babe, whose mother's breast
But a moment gave it rest.
Through the village churchyard, too,
While the graves were bright with dew,
Where the snowdrop hangs her head,
Primroses their fragrance shed,
And the birds their matins wake
Soon as day begins to break.
Over many a corpse-sown flood,
Over plains once red with blood,
Through the haunts where guilt holds breath
Passed the Lord of Life and Death,
With His banner all unfurled,
Come with healing for the world ;
He, the Victor in the strife,
Resurrection and the Life !

Yes, my King, the dead upraise Thee,
They gone down to silence praise Thee,

And the living service pay,
Quick and dead at one to-day,
Called the Paschal Feast to share :
O that we all keep it There,
Where nor death nor night is known,
Round about Thy Glory-Throne.

NIGHT AND MORNING.

PEACEFUL were the plains that night,
  Where the sheep lay sleeping ;
Stars shone out, like flowers of light,
  In the Angels' keeping :
Things seemed as they ever were,
  Since the fathers slumbered—
Suddenly, the cohort fair,
  Multitude unnumbered.

What the tidings that they brought
  To the royal nation ?
Wonder, which the Lord had wrought
  Through the Incarnation :
This they told, that God was born
  Of the Mother-maiden ;
Therefore leap the sad this morn,
  Rest the heavy-laden.

Clouds and darkness hie away,
   Light o'er earth is breaking,
Since the old law's sunset-ray
   Died last night, forsaking
Temple, sacrifice, and rite
   Of the ancient letter;
Old things past, the Lord of Might
   Brings us new and better.

Yesterday for thee, poor world,
   But to-day for Jesus:
Pride and scorning down are hurled,
   'Tis a Babe Who frees us.
Dreary years of waiting past,
   Now is come salvation,
Peace, Goodwill, and, wrought at last,
   Reconciliation.

SUMMER MORNING.

OVER field and over wold,
  Daylight breaks ;
Over village, over fold,
  And awakes
    Slumberers to life,
    Peaceful ones to strife.

Proudly in his regal march
  Comes the sun,
Gilding tree and spire and arch
  One by one ;
    Waking birds to song,
    Giant, swift and strong.

Bridegroom from his chamber fair,
  Come to bear
Over sea and over land,
  In his hand

Gifts of life and grace,
Changing Nature's face.

Every laughing little rill
    Seems to fill,
Every torrent, as it sweeps,
    Boils and leaps,
        Roaring, seems to say,
        " I am mad to-day !"

Now, too, all the solemn trees
    In the breeze
Greet the morn with stately mien,
    But the green,
        Young things fairly bound
        With many a cheery sound.

Cottages look thatched with gold,
    Gems untold
Are the dew-drops filled with light,
    Pure and bright :
        And the fleecy mist
        Hies, by sunbeams kist.

On the hill top, in the vale,
   Shadows pale;
Clouds and vapours sail away,
   For the Day,
     Vanquisher of Night,
     Hastes on wings of Light!

THE WATERS OF BAPTISM.

I STOOD beside a lake whose placid breast
   Told of unfathomed depth.   It scarcely moved,
   And mirrored there, surrounding things I proved;
Trees, flowers, and tints which flecked the glowing
      west.
   And as I watched there came a dove-like bird
   Which hung in air and then with pinion stirred
The quiet deep : quick, widening evermore,
A circle spread until it reached the shore.
So broods the Blessed Spirit o'er the font
   Of Baptism, troubling the slumb'rous wave
Where clearly pictured lies our piteous want :
   So, all embracing Love, which all would save,
From its blest Centre, spreads to utmost earth,
Bearing to souls the gift of the New Birth!

THE CONVERSION OF ST. PAUL.

No law the Lawgiver may bind,
   No rule the Ruler stay :
Eternal Love its course pursues,
   And strongest hearts give way.

Here, weary years of pleading win
   The victory at last :
There, in a moment, at his crime
   The sinner stands aghast.

The still, small voice, the gentle strife,
   The sudden blinding blaze,
Are all alike the call to souls,
   One call in divers ways.

This will melts down at Christ's command,
   Like ice before the sun ;
That, at His word, springs up to life,
   And thus God's Will is done.

And e'en from persecution's paths,
  Some haughty ones are led
To where, across their angry souls,
  The Light Divine is shed.

Then all is changed : the foe becomes
  The friend and advocate,
And love for Jesus takes the place
  Of slaughter-breathing hate.

This only grant, O Lord of all,
  That called to do Thy Will,
By years of slow, hard discipline,
  Or blow which strikes us still.

We listen, and Thy word receive,
  Nor dare to turn away
When Jesus speaks, and smites the heart
  With Love's consuming Ray.

DESIRING A CERTAIN THING OF JESUS.

"IF thou wilt my disciple be,
Leave all and follow Me,
  Father and mother, friend."
Jesus, we hear Thy gentle call,
We will arise, forsaking all,
  Be Thine unto the end.

Only we ask our sons may stand
Good Lord, at Thy right Hand,
  And on Thy left, when Thou
Dost reign, Thy kingdom made complete,
Thine enemies beneath Thy feet,
  Where we, Thy suppliants, bow.

And yet we know not what we ask
Of Him, Whose highest task
  To serve, though Chief of all:
His baptism, His cup to drink!
Ye who are able, fear to shrink,
  And daring, fear to fall!

14

A CAROL OF DAVID AND GOLIATH.

GOLIATH in armour is clad for the fight,
He hastes in his raging with furious might;
In pride and in prowess he comes like a flood,
He longs for the battle, is thirsting for blood.

One blow and the shepherd shall fall to the ground,
Goliath has never the vanquished been found;
He laughs at the stripling who dares him alone,
And scorns in his madness the sling and the stone.

The stripling shall master the giant ere long,
For God chooseth weak things to baffle the strong;
Five stones David takes him to hurl at his foe,
And one God electeth to lay the proud low.

More fierce than Goliath the foe of mankind,
Who God's ransomed children in fetters would bind;
But come he as demon, or angel of light,
The Sign of our Master shall put him to flight.

Yes! one as a thousand shall meet him alone,
And challenge the giant with sling and with stone;
The feeble the strongest in Gath shall pursue,
The strong man shall cower, the faint shall pursue.

A greater than David hath come to the fray,
The chambers of darkness are filled with dismay,
For Satan, Goliath of Hell, is cast down,
And Christ, Son of David, hath won the renown.

He strove in His meekness, He warr'd in His Might,
One sweep of His Arm, the smooth stone was sent
     right;
It sank in the forehead, and vengeance was sweet,
The foe of Jehovah lay slain at His Feet.

BEING HATED WITH CHRIST.

BUILT upon the true Foundation, Jesus Christ the
    Corner-stone,
Glorious, compacted nation, Thou the Ark of
    God alone !

All thy children, sons and daughters, from the
    land of Egypt free,
Through the flood, the Red Sea's waters, pass
    sweet Canaan, into thee.

Angels from God's presence flying, keeping not
    their first estate,
Bound in chains, in darkness lying, as the judgment
    they await :

Hard impenitency, weeping as the gnawing flame
    mounts higher,
Sodom and Gomorrha, reaping vengeance of eter-
    nal fire :

Those who, of the flesh defilers, all dominions
  despise ;
Of the priests of God revilers, evil speakers, loving
  lies :

These without, O chosen Nation! where the way
  lies smooth and wide,
But within, the salutation, " Peace and love be
  multiplied !"

" If the world despise and hate you, this your consolation be,
Not that peace and crown await you, but that first
  it hated Me."

Evil angels, impious sinners, world without, O hate
  us well :
Hate, with Jesus we are winners, love, and we are
  doomed to hell.

THE SACRED HEART.

O SACRED Heart of Jesus,
    To thee, to thee I turn :
Since thou for me, unworthy,
    With love Divine dost burn.

O Sacred Heart of Jesus,
    Before the living fire
Which fills thy Human Nature,
    I cast each vain desire.

Burn up, O Heart of Jesus,
    Each adverse will and thought :
This heart of stone be broken
    Before thee, as it ought.

O Sacred Heart of Jesus,
    Broken for love of me,
Some lowly, contrite token,
    Let my heart give to thee !

ST. CLEMENT, B. & M.

Nov. 23.

CLEMENT, thee whose name is written
  In the book of life, we sing,
Fellow-worker with th' Apostle,
  Fellow-servant of the King:
We the fight are still maintaining,
  Waging war till life be o'er,
Thou hast passed the Jordan waters,
  Thou hast gained the further shore.

With the Shepherd interceding
  For the flock He feeds below,
Holy pastor, faith beholds thee
  In the peaceful valley's glow:
If His rod and staff but comfort,
  If His Presence stay us here,
Who shall dread the valley's shadows?
  Who the powers of evil fear?

In Thy Book our names are written,
  Jesu, wipe them not away:
With the saintly cohort own us,
  When shall break the endless Day:
Thou Who here each soul dost shelter,
  Each by his own name dost call,
First, within Thy Fold to please Thee,
  Then to win the Heavenly Hall.   Amen.

JOHN HODGES, PRINTER, CHURCH STREET, FROME.